THE MAN IN
MY CHAIR

A NOVEL
by
H. B. KAYE

THE BOOK CLUB
121 CHARING CROSS ROAD
LONDON, W.C.2

THIS EDITION 1950

Printed and bound in Great Britain by
Novello and Company Limited, London, W.1

ONE

I

It was a fine clear night and I decided to walk home.

The air was warm, yet not too warm to be pleasant. Gently it caressed my face as though telling me how good it was to be alive. As if I did not know!

Above the stillness of the night itself I could hear the throbbing heart of the city; I could even smell its indefinable smell. Night in the city. Lovely city. *My* city.

I was drunk—not with liquor but with the heady, bubbling wine of success. That night was the climax of my career. My fellow-citizens had set the seal on all that I had achieved so far; they had given a dinner in my honour, a highly successful dinner. Everyone of importance had been there.

As I walked my thoughts whirled delightedly along, recalling the scene at the dinner, the good fellowship, the things that had been said about me, the compliments on my shrewdness, my sagacity, my zeal, my ability and my sense of citizenship. Again I heard the congratulations of my friends, and the applause with which my speech was received. Well, it had been a good speech and many times poor Janet had listened to it whilst I paced up and down the bedroom rehearsing it.

Despite my years I felt happy and excited, exhilarated. I was like a boy again. That night was mine alone: I would not share it with the troubles of the world; that night nothing could make me unhappy or despondent.

The majestic door of my town house confronted me

and I stood for a moment taking a last deep breath of that lovely, balmy night air.

Johnson, the butler, was waiting up for me. With his simple dignity he offered me his own congratulations and hoped the evening had been a success.

" A great success, thank you, Johnson. An evening I shall not forget."

" I have put the whisky and some sandwiches in your study, sir."

" Thank you, Johnson. I won't want you any more."

" Very good, sir. Mrs. Price asked me to say that she would be awake if you would like to see her before you went to bed."

That was nice of Janet. She knew I would want to tell here about the dinner. How rotten for her to be ill on a glorious night like this !

Johnson moved over to the door. " Good-night, sir."

" Good-night, Johnson."

Humming to myself I glanced in the mirror as I passed, then stopped to take a good look. I tried to see myself detachedly that night but perhaps I was biased a little in my own favour ; it was to be expected. I saw a medium-sized man, hair still dark though slightly greying at the sides, face firm—(were those pouches under the eyes?)—a neat moustache over the determined mouth and chin. Yes, a strong face but one used also to laughter and good humour, I hoped. The figure not too bad ; not exactly athletic, perhaps, but still with only a slight paunch—scarcely perceptible if I held myself erect.

I winked at the fellow in the mirror as I turned away and made for the study. After all it was not every day that one could feel complete self-satisfaction, in perfect harmony with life.

I would stay a few minutes in the study, savouring the sweet moment, and then I would go up to see Janet.

At the threshold a sudden sharp pain shot through my chest and for an instant I felt dizzy and stumbled. Then my head cleared and all was well again. I shook my head and smiled to myself; perhaps the excitement had been a little too much. But I forgot about it when I stepped into the study, my own comfortable, familiar room—the great desk, the walls lined with books. I was filled with sheer contentment.

I went across and touched the small carved head of my daughter Elizabeth. It smiled at me.

And then I heard his deep voice for the first time. It was courteous and well-spoken, yet I thought I detected in it a faintly sardonic flavour.

" Good-evening, Mr. Dexter Price."

I confess I was startled ; I had every reason to be. I had thought I was quite alone and then suddenly— the voice! I jumped and turned round, my thoughts filled with visions of a burglar, an assassin. . . .

But the man I saw was neither of these. He was tall and handsome—in a florid way—and dark eyed. Yes, those eyes seemed dark but, more than that, they were penetrating. One reads of penetrating eyes without fully comprehending. I had never seen eyes like these before ; they seemed to search my very soul. And there he was—calmly sitting in my chair, the lovely, high, carved chair that I had found in Florence.

" Good-evening," I said when I had recovered. " You gave me quite a fright. I can't understand Johnson forgetting to tell me there was someone here." It was annoying of Johnson, too, to have shown a stranger into my study and left him there with all my private papers.

" Johnson," he said in his deep voice, " did not see me come."

I frowned. " I'm afraid I don't understand. How could you come in without his knowing? "

" I did not come," he replied. " I *arrived*."

The very calmness and assurance of his voice lent the emphasis a peculiarly sinister inflexion. But by now I had fully recovered my equanimity ; nothing should disturb it on that night, I repeated to myself, nothing.

" You're playing with words," I told him good-humouredly. " Very well. Let us say you did not come here but you—*arrived*. You did, I suppose—um—*arrive*—by the front-door? " I went over to the decanter. " Will you join me in a drink? "

" Thank you," he said, " but I don't drink. No, I did not use the front-door."

" Well, that's odd." I poured out a drink for myself. " For some reason, then, you came in through the tradesmen's entrance. Extremely careless of the servants to leave it open. Still—"

I turned to face him and took a sip of the whisky. His eyes were fastened on mine and his tone was deliberate.

" I did not come through any door. Nor," he added as an afterthought, " through any window."

I lowered my glass. " Oh, come, my dear fellow ! A joke's a joke ! Let's not be too absurd. You'll tell me next you're a ghost or something."

I drank off the whisky and smiled at him, waiting for his reply. He did not speak, however, only looked at me with those extraordinary eyes.

After a while my smile went. I was beginning to feel embarrassed under his scrutiny, to feel ridiculously inferior. And I did not like it. And then the lights seemed to be getting dimmer and at the same time I was growing angry.

" Well, why don't you answer? " I said rudely. " What do you want here, anyway? "

The spell of dizziness was returning ; that would account for the seeming dimness of the lights. The evening had been too much for me. I must go to bed. And still the man kept on staring at me. He would have to go away ; I would see him in the morning.

His voice broke through my spinning brain. " Sit down," it commanded. " Sit down and look at me."

And in my own house, too, my own room ! He even sat there in my chair . . .

But I was feeling too unwell to argue with him, to point out that it should be I who was asking *him* to sit down. I collapsed into a chair and held my hand to my head.

" You will feel better in a moment," he said. But I could detect no sympathy in his tone ; it was more in the nature of an order. Indeed my head did begin to clear but the lights still remained dim.

The man stood up. He was taller than I had thought. Round him he wore a cloak which, though sadly out of date, somehow suited his dark, flashing manner. There was a nobility about him, a sense almost of beauty. In that room grown dim he gave the impression of radiating his own light. There was about him an indescribable inner glow.

" So you really do not know who I am? " he asked.

I gazed at him, unable to tear my eyes away from those terrible ones of his. He pulled back his cloak and involuntarily I gasped. It was as though I were looking at an X-ray picture ; his bones showed white and translucent through his flesh, through his clothes. His face too now showed a skeleton behind the flesh and hair, only those eyes burning me from their sockets.

I was shivering and feverish in my chair and as the truth assailed me I own that I tried to crouch miserably away from that apparition.

"Yes, you—you are—" I began. But I stumbled before that word and could not utter it. I licked my dry lips. "Your name is *Death*," I whispered and I held my hands up to my eyes as if to shut that figure out. But it was still there when I dropped my hands.

Death let his cloak fall into place and stretched out an arm towards me. "Come," he said. "I am waiting for you."

Some force beyond mine was urging me up towards him. But I clutched at the arms of the chair. "No," I said. "No, I'm not ready for you yet. Don't you understand? I'm not ready to die."

The full meaning of the situation was sweeping over me. I had never been afraid of dying but this sudden visitation had taken me by surprise. I did not want to go yet. My time could not be up ; there was still so much to do. I determined to fight for my life, to plead . . . the thing was not yet irrevocable.

"Please," I said. "Let me have a little more time, a few more years. You don't understand. To-night I have reached the climax of my career. Don't you see? I am an important man ; there is so much for me to do. I'm needed here. Just a few years. It can't make any difference to you. Surely you see that I shall be more use here ! I'm only just over fifty : it's not very old, is it? I know that no man is indispensable.

But then it takes a long time to work up to the position I've reached. And one does acquire a little useful knowledge on the way. Besides, look at my business. It's a large one, you know. I built it all up myself. And if I go now it will crumble because I've not had time to put my affairs in order. I don't want to stress it but I really am rather important—according to our little standards, of course. If only you could see your way! . . . Just a short time."

Death looked at me. When he spoke his voice was openly contemptuous.

"What good are you?" he asked. "You who are selfish, greedy, mean, possessive, conceited, cruel, lustful! What have you ever done for others in this world? What kind of legacy will you leave behind? What, I am asking, is the use of you that you think I should grant you more time?"

I must say I was considerably taken aback at this vicious onslaught. I had never claimed to be a paragon of virtues but all those things!—I was not going to sit down to that. My dossier must have got mixed up with someone else's.

"Oh, no," I protested firmly. "I think I can safely say I have never been any of those things. I've not been a saint by any means but I've nothing in my life to be ashamed of. I don't honestly think anyone would call me a bad man and I've tried to the best of my ability to live a good life. No, I've certainly nothing to be ashamed of."

"Do you mean," Death asked curiously, "that if you had your life to live over again, you would live it as before? Even with the foreknowledge you now possess?"

"I would not change one iota of it," I cried.

Death looked at me strangely. Then he sat down in the chair again. " Very well, then," he said at last. " You will have such an opportunity. You will live your life over again and we shall see what you think of it. Look inwards."

And suddenly there was a click in my brain and I was seeing a film of scenes in my own life projected clearly upon the screen of my mind. The room about me began to grow quite dark . .

2

I was a boy—about nine or ten. I saw myself walking down past the house. I remembered it quite well and I knew where I was going—towards the lawn. My new air-gun was tucked under one arm and Cæsar, our red setter, was on the end of a lead held in my other hand. When we reached the lawn I tied the dog to a tree. He looked up at me, wondering but quite trusting. I turned, stepped out exactly fifteen paces, turned again and raised the air-gun. As I took aim at the dog's centre I was filled only with curiosity . . .

" No," I said loudly, protesting. " It's not fair to start when I was a child. Most children are thoughtless and unkind at times. Surely you're not going to judge me by that now ! "

" All right," the voice said patiently. " It makes no difference to me where we start. Pick anywhere you like. What about the end of the first World War? "

I thought about that for a moment. Why not the war itself? My record was a fairly good one and there were one or two incidents I was proud of. But war creates exceptional circumstances and there were

also one or two incidents that were not too good.
They were excusable, I thought, because of the war
but it might be as well to start in more normal times.
The end of the war should be a good starting place.
I had met Janet then and we had got married ; there
couldn't be much wrong about that period, anyway.

"Yes, the end of the war," I agreed and the screen
in my mind lit up again. I wanted to sit back and
relax but I couldn't because I was too concerned with
what was happening there before me.

I saw a young man hailing a cab on Main Street.
Was it Main Street? Yes, surely . . . but those
buildings ! Of course—that was how it was almost
thirty years ago. Good heavens ! How one forgets !
And the young man—was that really me? Yes, much
the same but younger in every way ; the moustache
was already there but the carriage a bit more erect,
the step a little lighter, the eyes eager, in tune with
the world, glad just to be alive.

I had a grip with me; must be going somewhere,
then. A cab pulled up. Listen ! What was I saying
to the driver? Ah, yes, Central Station. A train
journey, obviously. Where to? I couldn't remember
for the moment but I would know soon.

The scene jumped. How like a film this was : one
had no control over events. Was that quite fair to slip
over the train journey? Perhaps something might have
occurred, something favourable to my case.

". . . You helped an old lady on to the train,"
Death said, reading my thoughts. " I'll make a note
of it if you like," he added sarcastically.

"Don't bother," I replied stiffly. "It isn't necessary."

So there I was, stepping out of the train with my

grip in my hand on to the platform of a small country station. It seemed familiar and suddenly I remembered and felt curiously excited. I was about to meet Janet for the first time. Only I didn't know it then, of course. In the " film ", I mean.

I handed in my ticket and walked out of the station, wondering if anyone would meet me and half expecting it. Yes, I remembered what was going on now. I was on a visit to the home of Joe Marsh. I was looking forward to seeing Joe again, too. When he'd been sent home I'd promised to look him up as soon as possible—and here I was at last.

Joe and I had been great friends in the Army. We'd seen a lot of war together and that binds people even if nothing else does. There was more to it than that, though. Joe and I took to each other from the start and along with the other thing, we'd had plenty of fun together. Not that he'd cared for girls very much, at least not as I had. Me, I'd liked them a lot. He wasn't stuffy about it and we often went out on double dates and had a good time, but with Joe that was all. He may have kissed one or two of them ; he certainly did no more. But then I'd always known he had a girl back home. And she was that sort of a girl, he'd said. If one had a girl like that waiting, one could wait, easily. I didn't know what he meant at the time ; I had never known a girl like that myself.

And then poor old Joe had to get smashed up. A nasty one, too. Through both knees—or, rather, it almost took the knees away. It was only a few months before the end of the war, though we didn't know it at the time. What a pity, I was thinking as I waited at the station, that Joe was so unlucky so near the end. They'd patched him up and sent him home.

It wouldn't be Joe meeting me, anyway!

But it looked as if no one at all was going to meet me. The other few passengers off the train had vanished and the station was deserted except for the ticket man. I went back to have a word with him.

Oh, yes, he said, he knew the Marsh family. He spoke respectfully of them and added gratuitously that they were nice people.

Well, how could I get there? I asked.

He scratched his head at that and reckoned I'd have to walk. About two miles it was. A pity it was so hot!

He took me to the door to direct me and put me on my way and just then a pony and trap came clip-clopping into view. The pony was hurrying all right but it pulled up short at the station and a girl jumped breathlessly down.

" Oh, dear, Mr. Jenks," she said to the ticket collector. " I've missed the train, I know I have. I did hurry as fast as I could but Betsy was being stubborn to-day. I had to meet a gentleman and take him back for Mrs. Marsh. You haven't seen him, I suppose? "

" Would I do? " I said, stepping forward.

" Oh! " she said, seeing me for the first time. Then timidly : " Are you Mr. Price? "

" Yes," I said. " That's me."

" Looks like you don't walk after all," said the ticket collector, giving me a wink.

The girl smiled nervously at me, then turned and walked to the trap. I followed. When she had climbed in, she sat looking expectantly at me. I handed up my grip and then climbed in myself. She was still looking at me and I looked back, a little impudently perhaps. Suddenly she broke her eyes away with a little sort of half-smile and snatched up the reins.

" Gee-up, Betsy," she said, jerking them sharply.

I sat gazing at her profile. It was pretty good to look at and somehow clean and clear cut. Her hair and eyes were dark brown. The eyes warm, the hair soft. But it was neither her features nor her colouring that were immediately so attractive ; the attraction lay rather in the air about her. Just to look at her was to glimpse something completely sincere and natural, something that took hold of one and instantly made the world a more desirable place to be in. She was a little below average in size. Yet there was a strength about her and this, I discovered later, went hand in hand with a refreshing trust in her fellow-beings.

It never struck me who she was and I imagined she might be Joe's sister—though he hadn't mentioned one to me.

" Mrs. Marsh asked me to meet you," she said. " There wasn't anyone else she could send and I haven't much to do just now, anyway."

Whenever her eyes met mine they flickered nervously away again.

After a minute's silence she glanced at me once more. " Why—why are you staring at me like that? " she asked breathlessly and then her face began to flush, the delicate colour spreading upwards and deepening. The effect was delightful but I looked away at that, realising that I had been embarrassing her. The kind of girls I had always known had enjoyed being stared at.

" Sorry ! " I said contritely. " Whenever I see a beautiful object I just stare ; I didn't mean to be rude."

My words drew up the receding flush again but I think she was rather pleased with what I had said.

I wondered at her use of the words " Mrs. Marsh ".

" Are you Joe's sister? " I asked, puzzled.

She laughed at the question, the laughter soft and low but friendly. " I should have introduced myself," she said. " My name is Janet Playfair."

Recollection stirred then and the day became suddenly darkened for me.

" You're the girl Joe was going to marry," I blurted out.

She nodded her head and corrected me. " *Is* going to marry. In a few weeks when Joe's a bit stronger."

" But surely," I protested, " now that he's—well, things can't be the same now."

" Why ever not? " she looked levelly at me. " Joe needs me more than ever now."

I didn't say any more but I thought how unfair it would be for a girl like this to be tied all her life to a cripple in a wheel-chair. I turned it over in my mind as we bounced along in the trap and the more I thought about it the more convinced I was that it would be wrong. I was deeply sorry for Joe but that was what war did to people. He was one of the unlucky ones. And surely if the girl was too loyal to break off the engagement then it was up to him to do so. Still, it was no good my thinking about it until I had seen Joe . . .

The girl told me that her family lived near Joe's and she and Joe had grown up together. " Fancy you thinking I was his sister ! " she laughed again. " But we were more or less like brother and sister until we grew up. Joe was always teasing me and pulling my pig-tails—why do little boys always pull little girls' pig-tails? Of course he's older than I am," She turned back to her driving.

" And what's Joe going to do now? " He had been studying medicine before the war.

" Do? " she echoed. " Well, I don't know." Then she said briskly. " But the first thing is to get him quite well again and then we can decide. His health is the important thing."

We drove up to the Marsh house then and I was impressed with what I saw. It was a large, quite imposing house with fine grounds. Obviously Joe's family had some money. Perhaps his career would not be so important after all.

His mother greeted me warmly. " We heard such a lot about you, Dexter," she said. " You don't mind my calling you Dexter? That's how Joe always talks of you. And he's been so looking forward to seeing you."

" How is he? " I asked.

" Quite well," she said. " The doctors have more or less finished with him now. They say they can't do any more for him. But he gets rather depressed at times, poor boy. It's only to be expected, I suppose." She shook her head doubtfully and looked at Janet. Then she said more brightly. " But perhaps seeing you will cheer him up."

" I'll do all I can to help," I said.

" And of course you've met Janet." She drew the girl towards her and put an arm round her. As they stood there together I could see there was a consider-able affection between them. " She's been so helpful : just like a daughter. I don't know what we'd have done without her."

Standing there together in front of the big-framed

timber house, they presented rather a striking picture. Shoulder to shoulder! As I watched the once played-out scene unfolding again I wondered for an instant if the older woman could have had some uncanny inkling of what was to come. But I dismissed the notion as fanciful. How could she have known? And in any case there was nothing she could have done about it, nothing anyone could have done. It just happened that way, that was all.

. . . "Did it?" Death broke in sardonically, reading my thoughts again.

I decided to ignore the remark. Obviously he hadn't taken the trouble to read up my case beforehand. But since he could apparently see into my mind as well as I could, he would soon find out how badly he had maligned me.

We went through into the house and there in the long hall was Joe waiting to welcome me. He sat in a wheel-chair; it was one that he could move along by himself. He did not come towards me, however, but waited for me to go across to him.

We shook hands warmly and greeted each other heartily, perhaps a little too heartily. Poor Joe looked very different from when I had last seen him. Normally his whole bearing conveyed a serene, good-natured disposition, a quiet confidence and pleasure in life. Now, however, his face was pinched and drawn. Evidently there was something troubling him badly quite apart from his physical injury.

"Well now, you two must have plenty to talk about," Mrs. Marsh said. "Why don't you take Dexter out to the garden, Joe, and Janet and I can make some ice cream and cold drinks and bring them out in a little while?"

" The garden? " Joe said doubtfully.

" Yes," I put in. " That sounds fine. Come on, let me push this contraption while I'm here. I can do with a bit of exercise."

" No," Joe said sharply. " I can manage."

I took my hand off the chair feeling rather piqued ; but I realised that he must hate to think he was constantly dependent on others. Janet was looking at me, pity welling from her, imploring me not to take offence.

" Good," I said. " I was only being polite. The thought of having to push a big lump like you around was really pretty shattering. How about showing me the way? "

As we moved off, I knew the two women were watching us and I knew, too, that Janet's expression had changed to gratitude. I wanted to turn and look at her but I didn't.

We went out of the french windows and I eased the chair down the single step on to the lawn. Joe scowling because he obviously couldn't manage it without assistance.

" What's biting you, Joe? " I asked. " You're not going to hold a grudge against the world just because you have to have a helping hand now and then, are you? "

" Well, it does make me feel pretty sick," he confessed. " If it was just for a while, it wouldn't matter a damn—but to be this way for always ! . . . It's a staggering thought to a fellow that's always been fairly active."

I pointed to the stumps of leg which were all of the injured limbs that remained to him. " Didn't they fix you up with new legs? " Not that artificial legs in those days were as good as they are now.

" Yes, I've got some," he said gloomily. " They're knocking around in a cupboard upstairs somewhere I don't fancy the things much. Sure, they gave me some crutches, too, but you don't catch me hopping round like a blasted bird." Bitterly he added : " A chair's all I'm good for and that's what I'm sticking to."

" Hell, I'm sorry you feel like that, Joe."

" Sorry ! That's all I ever get—pity and sympathy. What good's that going to do me? Won't find me any new legs, I reckon."

It was obvious that the whole thing had been preying too much on his mind. He'd been alone with it too long, thinking about it when he should have tried to turn his mind on to other things. I determined I would do my best while I was there to get him to be less introspective, to try to get his thoughts out of the morbid rut they were in now and on to a more constructive level. I would have to go slowly, though. No use in rushing things.

He must have misread my silence. He glanced up at me and smiled. " Sorry about that outburst, Dex. I know you didn't mean it that way. I guess I just take myself too seriously. But it's good seeing you again. It's given me a new fillip already. Why, do you know this is almost the first time I've been out in the garden for weeks. I don't like to come out usually, especially if I'm alone ; begin thinking about the times when I used to run around here."

At that he began to grow morose again but with an effort he brightened once more. " It's swell out here, isn't it? At the bottom of the lawn there's a stream. We used to dam it up when we were kids. Look, let me show it to you."

And briskly he wheeled his way across the lawn, for once forgetting his disability—or at least pushing it aside for the time being.

Mrs. Marsh and Janet seemed surprised to find us down there a little while later with Joe enthusiastically telling me about events from his childhood and youth that had happened there.

" Do you remember—" he turned to Janet and happily she joined in the game of reminiscence.

Janet stayed on for dinner that evening, so that there were five of us. The fifth, of course, was Joe's father.

Joe, in choosing medicine, had not been following his father's profession. Mr. Marsh was a lawyer and I believe he had a pretty good practice in the nearby town. He travelled there each day by car. His hair was thinning badly on top and he had a large beaky nose ; however, as his chin thrust forward to meet the nose it was not so noticeable as it might otherwise have been. For some reason I had expected him to be rather pompous ; he was, on the contrary, kindly and unassuming.

It was quite obvious during dinner that Joe was his parents' major concern in life and that they were both delighted to see him in what must have been an unusually cheerful mood since his return from the Army. He was still reminiscing, but now it was about the experiences he and I had shared. Our talk and laughter was infectious to the others and they all joined in with interjections and comments.

" And there was the Frenchy," Joe was saying, " trembling with fury. ' Please to say ', he yells, ' why you have been aiming shells at your own Allies? You might have killed us off, a whole Company, if they had but hit us.'

" ' Och, we're out of practice, me bhoy ', says Clive McTurk apologetically. ' Give us the range and we'll have another go. Sure, we'll not be missing you the next time.' "

Mr. Marsh laughed and clapped his son affectionately on the back.

To an outsider seeing that scene it would have appeared that things were going swimmingly. Yet there was a tension there and we all knew it. Behind the laughter and the talk everyone was looking covertly at Joe to see if he was still enjoying himself. And undoubtedly the object of these glances felt that the scene was being overplayed. Yet the girl and the two older people were so plainly glad to see him like that, that he had not the heart to drop back to his usual moodiness. And, gallantly, he played the scene out for the rest of the evening in the same key.

Before she went home, Janet found an opportunity to speak to me.

" You've done him so much good," she said softly. " I am glad you came."

Her large brown eyes were shining and for a moment I held my breath as I looked at her.

In that instant I fell deeply in love with Janet Playfair.

I did not then recognise the feeling in its entirety for I had never experienced it before. I did know that some strange alchemy was at work inside me and that everything had begun to take on a new significance. The sensation was half bitter, half sweet, and I stared at her, not understanding it. Perhaps she saw something of what I was experiencing, for she gave that little shy half-smile of hers and turned away.

The next day Janet was occupied with something or

other and did not appear.   She had intimated as much the night before.   At breakfast Mrs. Marsh said to Joe : " What are you going to do to-day, son? "

Joe looked at her.   " Do? " he repeated, looking puzzled.   He was so used to doing nothing but mope around the house day after day.

" Yes, surely you and Dexter aren't going to stay indoors all day in this fine weather.   You know what I think you should do?   Why don't you both take a drive in the small car?   I'm sure Dexter knows how to drive."

I don't think Joe was keen on being driven in his own car, but as I seconded the idea he gave in gracefully.   I thought it would do him good to get out and besides I wanted to have a few words alone with him.

We drove up into the hills in that old-fashioned, rather clumsy car and there was a small but welcome breeze up there.   Below we could see the thick woods leading to the valley.   I parked the car on one side of the road for a while.

" You haven't told me much about yourself, Dex," Joe said.   " What have you been doing since you left the Army and what are your plans?   You remember how we used to talk about the future and you said you weren't going to plan ahead because it might be a waste of time?   But you're in the clear now.   What's it to be? "

" Well, I've just been looking round," I answered. " I've got a small bit put by.   And there's the gratuity. Maybe enough to start a small something with.   I guess it'll have to be small to start with, but you wait and see—once I get started, I'm going places, Joe."

" Sure you are.   I wish I could go them with you. Maybe Dad could help you, Dex.   He's got a finger in quite a few pies. I'll speak to him if you like."

"Thanks. But what about you? You're still going ahead with medicine, aren't you? "

He looked across at me and gave me a crooked smile. " A fine kind of a doctor I'd make, wouldn't I? I'd hardly inspire confidence in my patients, I think, hopping up to them on crutches or panting along in my wheel-chair."

I shook my head. " You're taking this the wrong way, Joe. You should think about the fellows who got it much worse than you."

He cocked his head sardonically. " And where would that get me? What do you want me to do—get down on my stumps and thank God for being so kind to me? "

" All right," I said. " I'm not going to preach."

After a while I said : " Joe, there is one thing I'd like to ask you, and that's about you and Janet."

" Yes," he said. " What about me and Janet? "

His voice was not antagonistic but now I found it difficult to put what I was thinking into words.

" Well, it's just . . . well, she's a great girl, Joe."

" Yes," he said quietly. " I know she's a great girl."

" Maybe it's none of my business," I blurted out, " and I don't want to hurt you, but how is it between you now? I mean she told me you were still engaged. Surely you're not going to marry her, are you? "

Joe was sitting quite still but his hands were clenched tight. He stared straight ahead of him. When he spoke his voice was calm but taut, as though he was restraining something.

" We've been good friends, haven't we, Dex? "

" Sure we have," I said. " And always will be, I hope."

" And always will be," he repeated.   " So that
I can know for certain you're on my side."

" Of course I'm on your side, Joe.   You know how
I feel about you."

" Okay, then.   Now I want you to go ahead and
tell me what's in your mind."

I swallowed.   This was difficult.   " You mean about
Janet? "

" Yes.   And don't mind me.   I want to know what
you really think.   Honestly, you'll be doing me a
favour.   I've been doing too much thinking alone."

I looked at Joe and I thought of how he used to be
and then I saw him as he was now.   Then I saw Janet,
fresh and lovely, with her life before her.   And I saw
her tied behind Joe's wheel-chair for all the years to
come and I didn't like what I saw.

" It's no good, Joe.   Don't you know it's no good?
Oh, hell, I wish that things could be different for you.
But it wouldn't work out.   I guess she'd marry you
all right.   She's the kind of girl that always sticks to
her bargains and makes out she likes it.   She's the
loyal kind : it's easy to see that.   But you wouldn't
ask her to do it.   It wouldn't be fair to her.   She's
young and there's all her life before her.   It wouldn't
be right to . . . this is hard to say, Joe : I told you I
didn't want to hurt you.   But I guess you've thought
of all this yourself, anyway.   She ought to have freedom
and movement. You wouldn't want her to marry
you out of—pity, would you? "

Joe crashed his fist down.   " No, by God, I
wouldn't ! "

There was quite a long silence.   Then he spoke
again but his voice was calm once more.   " I've said
all this to myself a hundred times.   But sometimes

people think too much and it gets distorted, out of line. That's why I wanted to hear what you thought about it . . . You're right, she's a great girl isn't she? What about getting back now? "

As I went to start the car I said, not wanting him to feel too bad : " It's tough the way things turn out. It might as easily have been me instead of you. If there's anything I can ever do, Joe, just let me know. Any time. Always remember that."

" Sure ! " he said. " Start her up now, Dex, there's a good fellow."

We were both silent on the way back. Joe was obviously deep in thought and I didn't want to intrude.

Lunch was a gloomy affair, very different from the dinner of the night before. Mrs. Marsh tried to keep some sort of conversation going and asked us questions about our drive. But it was hard work and mostly it developed into a tête-à-tête between the two of us with Joe enveloped in a grim cloud of his own thoughts. I was disappointed because he seemed to have relapsed back to his old mood again.

Mrs. Marsh left us alone after lunch and Joe said : " I don't feel so good this afternoon. I don't want to be unsociable but maybe you could amuse yourself for a while. I think I'll go to my room." His room was downstairs, of course, to make it easy for him to use it.

" Of course, Joe, that's all right. I'll look after myself. Sorry you don't feel very well. Maybe you should have a rest."

" Yes," he said. " I think I'll do that," and he wheeled himself away.

" Poor Joe," I told myself, gazing after him. " It must be a tough thing to beat this feeling that nothing's worth while any more. But we'll do it together all right."

I pottered around the house for a time and then went out to the garden.

Joe had a small black Scotty named Toby. It seemed to be his constant companion and sat on his lap most of the time. Now, however, Toby came out to join me in the garden. He looked a little woebegone and his tail drooped between his legs. He had evidently been turned out and I wondered what he had done wrong.

The two of us swung lazily in the garden hammock for a while, the dog's head resting mournfully on his paws.

" Come on, Toby," I said at last. " Let's go for a stroll."

We went out and down the road and a little way along my heart began to beat faster ; there was a girl coming towards us and I was pretty sure it was Janet.

" Hullo there," she said, smiling and greeting me as an old friend. " And you too, Toby. What are you doing away from Joe? "

The dog gave a feeble wag of his tail.

" Joe's not feeling very sociable this afternoon," I told her.

She looked dismayed. " But he was so much better yesterday. I thought that with you here—"

" Doesn't seem to have worked out that way, I'm afraid. But give it time. He's bound to relapse now and then."

" I don't understand about Toby, though. He's never been that unsociable before."

" It'll work out," I said. She looked doubtful and I went on : " Anyway there's nothing you can do about it right now. Are you busy? "

" No—I was just going back home."

" Well, how about taking pity on a stranger and showing me the local sights? Toby was doing his best but he's a little dumb, poor fellow."

" All right," she agreed and the three of us strolled along together.

" I feel so helpless about Joe," she said. " If there was only something I could do ! "

" Maybe the best thing you could do would be to stay away from him for a while," I suggested.

" Oh, but why? I try to be as cheerful with him as possible."

" Yes, but did you ever think that in some way he might feel he's letting you down? And that he might be thinking of how it could have been between you? "

" No, I hadn't thought of that," she said slowly. And then : " Oh, but that's nonsense really—I mean, about him thinking of how it could have been. We're going to be married and be very happy." Her voice was firm. " And I shall try to make it up to him for all he's gone through. If only he'd try to help himself a little ! He could make himself use those false legs . . . Things seem so much worse to him than they are because he's so sorry for himself and so bitter. He seems to feel cheated somehow. . . . Still, it's easy to talk, isn't it? I daresay we'd be just as bad if it had happened to us."

My heart leapt towards her. She was so loyal and unswerving. She never realised what it would be like living with a cripple and particularly one so embittered. Or if she did realise it she steadfastly refused to let her mind dwell on it. Instead she made pretence that their marriage would turn out happily, that she would force herself to be all things to him and perhaps drive his bitterness away. I knew better. And though I

2

said nothing to her to tell her that I realised what she was trying to do, I decided that such loyalty deserved better things of life.

When I went back to the house, Janet came with me. I told her that I thought it would be better for her not to do so but she insisted.

Joe was in the sitting-room, in his wheel-chair.

" Hullo, Joe," Janet greeted him with tenderness in her voice.

" Hullo," he growled back, not even looking up.

" I met Mr. Price along the road and we went for a walk."

" His name's Dexter," Joe said irritably. " You don't have to be so formal."

Janet glanced at me and shrugged her shoulders helplessly.

Just then I heard Toby whining and scratching at the door and I went to open it. The small dog tore across the room and hurled himself on to Joe's lap. Joe pushed him off. Again Toby jumped up and again Joe pushed him off, this time more forcibly.

" More damned pity ! " Joe exclaimed. " Even a dog has to pity me. Keep him away from me, will you? "

Janet picked up the small, quivering dog and began to soothe him. " Don't be so silly, Joe. He just wants to be with you because you're his master, because he loves you. And you throw his affection back in his face ! You ought to be ashamed of yourself."

" Sure ! " Joe said, scowling. " Well, keep him away from me, that's all. Dogs and women ! "

" You *are* being silly, Joe."

" All right, all right, stop badgering me. I—I just don't feel good, that's all."

" I'm sorry," she said.   " Perhaps I'd better go now.
But I'll look in after dinner if you like."

Joe frowned.   " I don't want you to do that, Janet.
I'd really rather be by myself.   Why don't you and
Dexter go out somewhere together?   You could take
the car and maybe go dancing or something."

" Thanks," she said.   " I expect Mr. Pri—Dexter
can make his own arrangements.   Besides, I'm not
particularly keen on going out.   I'd much rather be
here with you."

" No, Janet, I mean it.   I'd like to be alone.   I
know you'll understand ; or just put it down to my
general fatheadedness."

I turned to the girl.   " If Joe really feels that way,
I'd be very happy to take you out, Janet."

She stared for a moment at Joe.   Then she bit her
lip.   " All right," she said.   " I'll go and change."
And without another word she went out, still holding
Toby who was licking her arm.

After a while Joe said : " I'm afraid it isn't much
fun for you, being here.   I'm sorry—I keep trying,
but it isn't any use."

" Don't worry about me," I said.   " It's you I'm
concerned about.   You'll have to snap out of it somehow.   I only wish I could help."

" It'll help if you look after Janet for me.   I've got
to get things sorted out.   Sooner or later I've got to
make a decision ; I know I can't go on like this.   And
when I've made it, right or wrong, I'll take a stand on
it.   But I haven't got there yet.   So if you can look
after Janet for a while it'll give me a chance to get
things straight."

" I'll be glad to do that for you, Joe," I told him.

As I went to the door he said : " Dex, I—I suppose

it would be wrong to hold Janet to marrying me, wouldn't it? "

" I think you know the answer to that," I told him quietly but firmly.

He swallowed. " Yes. Yes, I guess so," he said.

3

I went in search of Mrs. Marsh and told her how things stood.

She sighed helplessly. " I don't know what we're going to do," she said. " It's a terrible blow for the poor boy, of course—but it's not as if he's the only one who got wounded. Others get over it—adapt themselves to a new way of life. I wonder why he's taking it so badly. And he must be better off than some of them, too. After all, he doesn't have to worry about money just at present and then he has Janet. She's a fine girl and she'll do her best to make him happy."

I nearly asked her : " What about Janet's happiness? " but I realised it was no use arguing about a thing like that ; Mrs. Marsh was a mother and as such was bound to be prejudiced in her son's favour to some extent. I could see that she was tormented by a desire to help and at the same time frustrated because she felt so helpless.

" Anyway," I said, " we can't force ourselves on him and I'd better do as he asked me. Things may improve in a day or two. But perhaps in the circumstances you'd rather I didn't stay? "

" Oh, no," she said. " He might be even worse if you weren't here. Besides, you can at least keep Janet from feeling too upset; I don't want her to spend all her time worrying."

"Very well," I agreed. "Then I shall do just what Joe suggested and take her out this evening. May I borrow the car?"

"Of course. Oh dear—it is all so upsetting." She was shaking her head as she went away.

Janet and I had quite a pleasant dinner in the town nearby although she was pretty quiet and her mind was obviously elsewhere. But afterwards we went on to some place that the waiter had told me about and we danced; and here she seemed to make an effort to put her thoughts on one side and suddenly came alive.

For me that evening with Janet was full of magic. Every second I was with her I fell more and more headlong in love with her; and to feel her close to me while we were dancing was an excitement that could scarcely be borne without confessing how I felt.

Of course, I did, in fact, tell her nothing of my feelings, but I could not keep the admiration from my voice, from my eyes.

And at the end of the evening, when I saw her home, she thanked me warmly for her enjoyment and pressed my hand for a moment. It was all I could do not to put my arms round her and confess what had happened to me in the short time I had known her. But that moment was not yet at hand.

During the next two days or so, Janet and I spent a good deal of time in each other's company. We were both rebuffed by Joe and, though I did not pride myself that she sought me out as I sought her, I think she felt that someone ought to entertain me and, as Joe couldn't bring himself to do so and Mrs. Marsh was too busy, she decided to give her spare time up to me.

We crammed a great many things into those two or three days and, though the spectre of Joe's unhappiness accompanied us everywhere, we did enjoy ourselves enormously. At times Janet would abandon herself and wholeheartedly fling herself into whatever we were doing—dancing, walking, driving or just laughing. And then suddenly would come the recollection of Joe and on the instant the laugh, the enjoyment on her face, would die away . . . Poor girl ! What a dreadful thing loyalty could be, I thought. And I, too, was continually conscious of Joe's unhappiness. If only he could have borne his misfortune and made light of it—how much less he would have suffered !

When I went home with Janet one evening she invited me inside for a few minutes and I met her mother. Her father was dead. Mrs. Playfair was about the same age as Joe's mother, but a very small person. Yet, in spite of her size, she was full of vitality and with it she was charming and sincere—a reminder here of Janet. White-haired she was, but her eyes twinkled with youthfulness of spirit.

" It'll be a sad day for me," she said, " when my daughter gets married." But her eyes were laughing. " What will I do with myself all day in a house to myself? I shall have to fill it somehow, won't I? Perhaps I'll fill it with babies. Will I? " she asked Janet. " But there, no need to blush, dear. Joe's a fine boy and he'll make you a fine husband. We'll soon have all this morbid nonsense out of his head. Marriage is what he needs." And she laughed, a delicious trill of a laugh.

Though I couldn't agree with her, yet her laughter was infectious and her gaiety could put anyone in a good temper.

Janet came out to say good-night to me and she was bubbling with a contagion of her mother's merriment. In the hall she began to dance and then whirled round and fell backwards into my arms laughing.

With her face looking up into mine I could not help myself and bent to kiss her.

That moment for me was magical but I only kissed her lightly. I saw her expression begin to change but before she could say anything I spoke quickly. "Just the end of a perfect day, Janet. Thank you for coming with me."

She stood up smiling, accepting the kiss merely as a token. "It has been fun, hasn't it?" Then her face clouded. "But I feel so guilty when I think of Joe. What a shame the poor darling has to miss all this."

I knew she deliberately used the word "darling" to remind me that our kiss had altered nothing, that she was still irrevocably bound to Joe. And I respected her for it.

"But I hope mother's right—about marriage. I will make him happy. I will."

I stood looking at her for a moment. Then I touched her hand. "Good-night, Janet," I said.

"Good-night," she echoed as I went.

When I went into the house everything seemed quiet but a light was still showing under Joe's door. I hesitated for a while, then I knocked gently.

"Come in," Joe's voice said.

He had not yet gone to bed but was in his wheel-chair. His crutches were beside him so that he could manage by himself when he wanted to go to bed.

I was surprised at his appearance. He looked better than I had seen him since my arrival. The lines in his face had eased out and the strained look had left him, leaving him calm and apparently untroubled.

"I'm glad you came in, Dex," he said. "I was hoping you would. In fact, I've been waiting up for you."

"I wanted to see you too, Joe," I blurted out quickly, not being able to contain myself. "Look here, when are you going to tell Janet? You can't just let her go on like this. It's not fair to her."

Joe looked at me. "You seem very concerned about her suddenly."

"Yes—well, it's because I've been seeing so much of her, I suppose," I said hesitantly. "She keeps talking about the marriage and—"

"What does she say?"

"Oh, she's going to do her best to make you happy and try to make up to you for everything, and so on."

"And so on, and so on!" Joe repeated almost to himself. Then he said: "As a matter of fact that's what I wanted to talk to you about, so at least our minds seem to be attuned to the same subject. Sit down, Dex."

I did so and he went on. "I told you I had to think things out and come to a decision. Well, I've done that. Now, tell me something. Are you fond of Janet?"

I coloured a little. "Yes, I am," I said.

"Are you in love with her?"

"Yes, I guess so."

"I see. Well, that makes things easier in a way. Have you told Janet how you feel?"

"Hell, no! What do you think I am?" I protested.

" So you don't know how she feels about you? "

" No—and she's too loyal to say anything, anyway, almost too loyal to allow herself to feel anything. But I think she would feel the same way about me if—if . . ."

" Go on, say it. If I wasn't in the way."

" Damn it, Joe," I said angrily. " I'm not trying to take your girl away from you. I wouldn't say a darned thing if you two were really going to get married. But you agreed it wasn't fair—"

" That's all right, Dex. Don't get excited about it. I'm not blaming you. Janet's an attractive girl. Besides, I'm glad this has happened, that's what I hoped for."

" And you'll tell her, then? " I asked eagerly, getting up.

" Everything will be all right," he said. " Don't worry about it."

I lay awake for a long time thinking about Janet and wondering if she would marry me and I lived over again in my thoughts the moment when I kissed her. Finally I went to sleep to dream that Joe was beating me on the legs with his crutches.

The next day was fine again. At breakfast I was glad to see that Joe was still looking as well as he had the night before. There was something added, a faint, almost imperceptible note of tension, of heightened awareness, but I did not pay much attention to that. Mr. and Mrs. Marsh noticed the improvement in him at once and though they were too sensible to speak about it, their reaction was quite apparent in their sudden cheerfulness. It was like the sun breaking through and dispersing a heavy bank of grey clouds, with the immediate lightening of everyone's spirits.

More surprising still was it when Joe suggested that

we all went for a picnic. Mrs. Marsh was delighted,
and though she excused herself from the excursion she
instantly made plans for Joe, Janet and myself to go.
They argued for a while where the best place was to
go, but Joe was insistent upon driving down to the coast
so that, he said, we ought to start as early as possible.

Immediately after breakfast I went over to warn
Janet to get ready. She was excited because it seemed
to mean that Joe was beginning to take an interest in
things again. I, for my part, wondered if he was going
to make an opportunity to talk to her that day. I
hoped so because the sooner the farce of their prospective marriage was over the better I would like it. I
was glad, of course, that Joe had at last come to terms
with himself and was obviously feeling so much better
and I hoped that he would now be able to find some
measure of happiness.

At last we were all set and I helped Joe into the car
Janet sat beside him and I took my place at the wheel.
Mrs. Marsh waved good-bye to us and we were off.

Joe knew that part of the coast pretty well and we
came along the cliff road and down to a small, quiet
beach. We left the car in the road after I had turned
it ; it seemed all right there. Then I helped Joe out
and he took his crutches, which he had brought with
him and followed Janet down to the beach. I brought
up the rear with the picnic basket.

It was a good lunch and Mrs. Marsh seemed to have
achieved the impossible at short notice. Cold chicken
and ham and pies and sandwiches and apples and
bananas.

It was warm and peaceful there and we lay back
contentedly for a while afterwards listening to the
eternal music played by the sea.

Then Joe sat up. "It was a wonderful lunch. Thank you, Janet."

"But I didn't make it," she said. "Or very little of it."

"I meant thank you for being here." Then he turned to me. "I'd like to tinker with the car for a while, Dex. I think it needs tuning up a bit. I wonder if you'd come and start her up for me."

"Of course," I said, and got up and helped him up. Janet was beginning to clear away the debris, her head bent over the things she was collecting together. I remember thinking what a pretty picture she made and then I looked up to find that Joe too, was staring at her. He was staring hard and almost like a sightless man. Then he put his crutches under his arms and turned away. But it was more than just turning ; it was almost as though he was *tearing* himself away.

We went up to the car and Joe got into the driver's seat and then I started it up for him with the handle.

"That's fine," he called to me. "I can manage now. You go on back and I'll join you in a while."

"All right," I said, and left him to it.

I helped Janet clear things up and then we sat down again and talked desultorily, Janet saying she wished we'd brought our bathing costumes, but that in any case there was nowhere to change, and I wondering what she would look like in a costume. And then suddenly the roar of the engine seemed to break in on us both simultaneously and we looked round.

The car was beginning to move.

I gave a startled look at Janet and then jumped up and ran across. But I was too late and the car moved smoothly past me. Joe saw me and waved once and then he was away.

Janet joined me. " How did he do it? " she said, almost in a whisper. " How can he drive without any legs? "

I shrugged my shoulders. I was as much at a loss as she was. We never did find out for certain, but I think he must have managed it with the aid of one of his crutches. It would be just possible for a determined man and there were the hand throttle and brake to simplify matters. The clutch was the only difficult part.

But why? And then I realised I had said it aloud and added : " I suppose he wanted to prove to himself that he wasn't so helpless after all. He'll be back in a few minutes, I expect."

" I hope so," Janet said uneasily.

We went back to the beach and I thought out a few jokes to make about Joe's venture when he returned. But half an hour passed and there was no sign of him, and then an hour.

" Surely," I said, " he hasn't gone off home and left us to get back on our own ! "

" It's not that I'm worried about," Janet said. " I'm hoping he hasn't had an accident."

We stayed there looking at each other, not knowing what to do. And then we heard a car coming and ran up to the road. But it was not the right car.

The man who was driving stopped when he saw us. He was a large, hearty individual with a great moustache.

" Can you tell me where I can find the police in this one-eyed place? " he boomed at us. " A fellow's had a nasty accident way back."

I did not dare to look at Janet, but I heard the little cry she gave and I felt my own stomach contract.

" Accident ! " I said. " Who was it? Where? Was it a car? "

" That's right," he said, looking up at me. A car. Right over the top of the cliff. About a couple of miles away. Don't know who he is."

Janet described the car and then Joe.

" Not much of either of them left," the man said. " But that's him. Saw a broken crutch beside him. Friend of yours? " he asked curiously.

But Janet had burst into tears and her face was covered by her hands.

" Yes, a very great friend of ours," I said, putting an arm round Janet. " This is a terrible shock. I wonder if you'd be kind enough to take us with you to the police."

" Certainly, certainly," he said. " If we can find them. Hop in, will you? "

I helped Janet in and got in beside her. I held her tightly, realising what a dreadful blow it must be for her. She was sobbing terribly.

Yes, that was a hard time for Janet, and for Mr. and Mrs. Marsh. It was Janet who broke the news to his mother when all the ghastly business and the first formalities were over. She begged to be allowed to do it, and I was glad because that was something I just couldn't do.

Seeing it happen over again after all that time, I pondered for a moment on just how strange my companion's work was. Why should Death have called poor Joe out just when he had come to a decision to stand up to Life? It seemed so wasteful.

And then I saw two scenes in which I played no part whatsoever. I was taken right outside my own life.

In the first one I saw Joe inside the car. And I

saw him look over towards where Janet and I must
have been. Then his lips compressed, and he took
one of his crutches and manœuvred it on to the clutch
pedal. It slipped off once or twice but he persevered.
Then the car moved off.

It was frightening to see Joe using that crutch and the
tight, hard look on his face.

The car was retracing its steps—back along the way
we had come that morning. Along the narrow cliff
road it went. There was no one about as Joe
approached the bend. But he did not try to turn the
steering-wheel, only pressed his lips more tightly
together. He was going towards the edge and there
was nothing to stop him. It was dreadfully real and
I shouted frantically to him to turn away. But no
words came. His hand was not even touching the
wheel now ; he had set his course. And then he grinned.
" This is it ! " he said. And he whispered : " Good-bye,
Janet. Be happy ! " I could hear the love and tenderness in his voice. Then the car went hurtling over
and I sat back, limp, waiting for the sound of the
crash below.

But before that could come the scene changed and
I saw Janet, white-faced except for the redness of her
eyes, standing before Mrs. Marsh.

Joe's mother was looking at her and I could see the
old lady's eyes widening with a growing fear as she
stared at the girl.

" It's Joe ! " she said breathlessly at last and Janet
nodded.

" There was an accident. He took the car off by
himself. He went—he went over a cliff."

Mrs. Marsh stared incredulously at her. " Oh,
no ! " she said at last. " He's had so much already.

Surely they'd spare him that! . . . It can't be Joe.
It's a mistake." She sank down in a chair and then her
whole body began to tremble convulsively. "He's
dead," she whispered and Janet nodded again and
ran across to her.

I tried to turn away from that scene but of course
I couldn't.

After a while Mrs. Marsh said : " Perhaps he's
better off this way."

"Oh, he's not, he's not," Janet said passionately.
" I loved him so much and we would have been happy,
I know we would. Life's so unfair. From someone like
Joe it takes and takes and to someone like Dexter it
keeps on giving . . ."

And from that scene my mind limped away at that
point.

Mentally I felt bruised and stunned ; but inexorably
the life history went on. . . .

TWO

THE pictures began to pass quickly. It was almost like turning over the pages of an old photograph album.

There was one, grey and dismal, of all of us standing silently round a grave as the coffin containing Joe's remains was lowered into it.

Then there was one in brighter colours, of Mr. and Mrs. Marsh giving me a car. It was in memory of Joe, they said, and I had been his friend. And they hadn't wanted me to feel badly about my being there when Joe went off. . . . When I protested, they insisted. They wanted to do it ; they hoped it would be of use to me. What a charming kindly pair they were !

And there I was ready to go, standing beside my new car, and Janet was there to say good-bye to me.

I took her hand. " I shall miss you, Janet."

" And I shall miss you, Dex. I—I don't know what I'd have done if you hadn't been here to help me."

" Will you write to me, Janet? "

" Why, yes, if you'd really like me to."

" I'd like it very much," I said. I hadn't told her yet that I wanted to marry her. There were things to be done first and in any case she was not the kind of girl you could rush after what had happened.

She waved good-bye to me and I went back to my city and my small room in the house where I boarded. My parents were dead and, apart from a married sister a long way away, I hadn't any close relations. My mother had died when I was quite young and my father during the war. He had left me a little money and this, together with my gratuity, formed my small capital.

The first problem was to find something to do ; I'd been drifting around long enough and it was time to get down to something. The things I had been doing and the people I'd been seeing a good deal of seemed to have lost their savour since I'd met Janet. And the girls I knew had certainly lost their glitter somewhere.

The trouble was that I hadn't any particular leanings. My father had had a job with a big firm but it hadn't been a very good one and I had no ambition to follow in his footsteps. I thought sometimes of getting a small shop but I never became enthusiastic about the idea.

I was, however, rather mechanically-minded and I spent hours tinkering with my car and taking it to pieces and assembling it again. And then one day I saw a racing car for sale. Immediately I experienced a burning desire to own that car and race it. I thought about it and slept on the idea that night, but my mind had been made up the moment I saw it, and the next day I exchanged my new car for the racing model.

That car was my pride and joy and for the next few weeks I ran it in every race possible, sometimes getting nothing but the thrill out of the race and occasionally winning and taking the cash prize offered. Of course, racing in those days was hardly what it is to-day, but it seemed exciting enough then.

All this time I was writing to Janet, for I wanted her to remember me continually and I also wrote to her mother suggesting that she bring Janet to the city to give her a change of scene and help her to get over

Joe's death. I was delighted, then, to hear one day that they were really coming.

I booked rooms for them at a good hotel and then I could hardly contain myself waiting for the great day. Eventually it came and I was at the station half an hour before the train was due, fuming and fretting until it arrived.

It was wonderful to see Janet again. In my mind I had made a thousand false images of her and not one of them was as good as the reality. We were shy with each other until her tiny mother stepped beside her and said twinkling : " Well, I've come to see you, after all, Mr. Price, and Janet thought she'd better come to chaperone me."

What a mountain of luggage they had brought with them. I thought we should have to have a separate cab for it but we just managed to squeeze it in. . . . And then followed a whirl of places to which the three of us went. The days came and went, packed profusely with pleasure ; but their going was all too quick. One day I was racing and they came to see me ; it was a great day for me because Janet was there and I won. I had never driven better. Afterwards, I asked Mrs. Playfair if I could take Janet out dancing, to celebrate, and she looked at us both and smiled and said : " Yes, I dare say I could do with a rest to-night."

And this time when we were alone together, Joe did not come between us as he had before. Neither of us had forgotten him in any way ; we thought of him now with sad remembrance, but we knew that it was useless to bind ourselves to the past.

It was as we began to waltz that I decided the time had come—or rather that I could not wait any longer. Immediately a giant hand seemed to clutch at my stomach and I was filled with apprehension. Suppose she refused me? I might be mistaken and she might have no affection for me at all. My mouth became strangely dry.

Janet said dreamily: " I could waltz like this for ever."

Desperately I seized at it. " Will you? " I asked above the music.

She looked puzzled. " Will I what? "

" Will you—waltz with me for ever? "

She seemed surprised and I almost shouted at her: " Please Janet, will you marry me? "

Round and round we went. She said : " I think I'm getting dizzy. You did say 'marry', didn't you, Dex?"

I nodded. I couldn't speak.

" Now I am dizzy. Yes, Dex."

It didn't dawn on me for a few moments. Then : " You said ' yes ' ; you said ' yes '." I grinned at her and she was smiling shyly at me and I whirled her round faster and faster and faster. When the music stopped we were both laughing and out of breath.

" Let's go straight back and tell your mother," I said. I hoped she would have nothing to say against the marriage.

It was still early and Mrs. Playfair had not yet gone to bed. She looked alarmed when she saw us returning so soon and then she must have noticed our faces. " Well," she said smiling, " I see you have something to tell me."

" How did you know? " Janet asked, surprised.

" Not very difficult, dear. You want to marry her, Dex? "

I nodded. " I've just asked her and we came straight back to tell you."

" That was nice of you. Well, I've no objection, if that's what you're wondering. What Janet decides is good enough for me. Her happiness is all I care about and if you make her happy you have my blessing." She took hold of her daughter's hand. " Congratulations, both of you ! "

After a moment she said : " There's just one thing. When were you thinking of getting married? "

" We haven't discussed it," I said.

" Well, before you do, I think you ought to have a job or an occupation of some kind. You know what I mean. Don't be offended, Dex, but car racing isn't really suitable for supporting a wife on, is it? "

" No, I hadn't intended that. I've only been marking time. But I will find something now—now that I've got an aim in life." I was looking at Janet, feasting my eyes on her. I knew then that this was the beginning, that things were going to turn out well for me. Janet was the beginning and the symbol. I was going to be a success.

2

When they had gone back home I set to with a purpose. I bought every paper I could lay my hand on and read all the advertisements until my head ached. Then I went out for a stroll. On the way I passed the Turkish baths. I had never been inside but I suddenly felt I would like to go in. I needed to relax for a while and then after that I would come to some decision.

My clothes went into the locker provided and I stayed in the steam room for a while. Then I went into a small cubicle to cool off. I was lying there, not thinking about anything in particular, my mind and body relaxing, when I heard voices. They came from the next-door cubicle and I heard them quite clearly.

"Jack, there's something I've been meaning to ask you."

"Go ahead, Jeff."

"It's a touch, I'm afraid."

"Well, go on. No harm in asking. What's it for? Got a girl lined up?"

"No, this is serious, Jack. I've found the place I want. There's a garage at the bottom of Duke Street. McCall's."

"Yes, I know it. You mean it's for sale?"

"Sure. That's what I'm trying to tell you. McCall hasn't told anyone yet. Or so he says. But I happened to be in talking to him and we got on to it somehow. I was telling him how I'd like a place like that and he said he was selling. I thought he was kidding at first, but he means it. He's in trouble—his family or something—and he's got to get away quick."

"So you're going to buy it?"

"I'd like to, Jack. It's too good a chance to miss. That place is good. I've seen some of the trade he gets and he even showed me his books. And there's things could be done that would make it even better. I've got my gratuity but that's all I have and it's not quite enough. He can't give me a loan because he needs the cash. I thought maybe you could manage it ; it won't be for long."

By this time I was fully alert. A garage ! Why on earth hadn't I thought of it before? With my interest in cars that was the very place for me. Then the unseen Jeff mentioned the price and it was certainly not high. Probably the owner had done that deliberately so that he could sell quickly. I would be able to manage that figure even though it would practically clear me out.

Well, I made up my mind quickly ; that's one thing I've always been able to do.

Jeff was offering his friend a partnership but the other declined. " No thanks, Jack," he said. " I'm not looking for another job. But it sounds all right and I'll find that money for you. It'll take me a bit of time to get it together. Will first thing to-morrow do? "

I moved off at that point and hurried into my clothes. Then I went straight to the bank.

The cashier said : " This is a fairly big amount to take in cash, Mr. Price."

I agreed, saying that I wanted it for a cash transaction. He looked doubtfully at me but it was nothing to do with him and he paid the money out.

From there I went to McCall's garage. I found it easily enough though it was a place I hadn't been to before. I was pleased with it and saw that the unknown Jeff had not been exaggerating.

McCall, a short, stout man, was attending to a car and I waited till he had finished and the customer had driven off. Then I went up to him.

" Mr. McCall? " I asked.

" That's me," he said.

" I'd like to buy this garage."

He seemed astonished. " You'd what? "

" It is for sale, isn't it? "

" Well—yes, but I was expecting someone else . . . How did you know about it? "

" Oh, these things get around." I told him what I was prepared to pay, mentioning a price a little higher than I knew to be the sum he had asked.

He was in a quandary. " Could you leave it over for a short while? " he said at last.

" I'm afraid not. I'll pay you cash—" I took out my bank-notes—" but I must have immediate possession. Otherwise the offer's withdrawn."

I could sense his struggle. He knew that the other man was interested but perhaps he wouldn't come back! Perhaps he couldn't find the money! A bird in the hand . . .

He gave in at last as I expected he would. " Come into the office," he said.

That evening I became the proud proprietor of a garage. I wrote to Janet about it and told her to begin getting her belongings together.

And the following morning I faced a surprised young man who asked me for Mr. McCall.

" He isn't here," I told him.

" When will he be back? "

" He won't be back."

His eyebrows shot up and he looked startled. I felt rather sorry for him. It had been good business on my part to get in first but I realised it was hard on him to have his expectations dashed to the ground.

" I've bought the business," I explained gently.

" But—but—I don't understand. Mr. McCall said he hadn't told anyone else he was selling."

" You know how these things get around."

" Oh, hell ! " he said. " This beats everything." Then he looked closely at me. " Haven't I seen you before somewhere? "

" Maybe," I said pleasantly. " I live here."

He produced a pile of bank-notes. " Look ! " he

said.   " I've screwed together everything I can to buy
this business. And now it's sold."

" It's hard luck," I agreed.

Then suddenly he grinned. He had fair, rumpling
hair and his face when he grinned was boyish and
attractive. He wasn't very old, anyway, certainly
younger than I was.   " Well," he said, " that's how
it goes." He half-turned and then looked back.   " As
I can't be boss, how about giving me a job? "

" Do you mean it? "

" Yes. This place was a bargain. I won't be able
to afford anywhere else for a while. I'm a good
mechanic."   It was a flat statement, not a boast.
" What about it? "

McCall had managed the place with himself and a
boy. But he'd worked like a slave and, anyway, I had
ideas of expansion.

" I'll take you," I said.   " Come in, and we'll fix
it up.   What's your name."

" Jeff Wilson," said my new employee.

The next few weeks were a busy time. I had to get
the hang of the business—and it was the first real
responsibility I'd ever had—and also try to get the
place running well and smoothly. With McCall,
although he had made quite a success of it, things had
been too haphazard ; they had depended on his whims
and moods. But I wanted the work to be organized.
And so it was—and because of that, I believe, more
efficient.

Jeff Wilson was an enormous help to me. I was,
after all, only an amateur engineer and Jeff was by
way of being a professional ; it had been his work in
the Army. He was engaged to be married, he told

me, but his girl was ill quite a lot. I met her when she came along to the garage sometimes. Marjorie, her name was. She was a fair, pretty girl, but she never seemed very strong and her fragile appearance lent an air of unreality to her.

I found a small apartment where the rental was fairly reasonable. It wasn't anything special but it was bright and I thought it could be made quite comfortable. I thought about furniture and decided I would have to sell my car. That was a bit of a wrench but I argued that I'd soon be able to buy another one. It was quite enjoyable choosing the furniture, furrowing out the best for the money available. I hoped Janet would be pleasantly surprised.

All was ready at last—except for the bride. I wrote to tell her and to ask her when she was coming. She replied that her mother insisted on the wedding taking place down there. I didn't think much of that idea for several reasons. One was that I didn't like to leave my new business so soon after taking it over ; another was that I felt that the memory of Joe would hover too much over a wedding there : willy-nilly it would affect both Mr. and Mrs. Marsh—who would naturally be invited—and, most important, Janet herself ; finally, I thought it wouldn't be promising for our marriage to start with Janet's mother insisting on anything.

I expected that Janet would back up her mother but I determined to have my own way and I wrote rather forcefully, merely giving the first reason and saying that it would mean at least three days away from the business and I couldn't manage it at that stage. I said we would just have a quiet, civil marriage and that I knew she would understand. I added that

I would expect her in two weeks and we would be married straight away.

Then her mother wrote :

. . . Janet says you are very obstinate—as if I couldn't see for myself—but it looks as if you're going to have your own way.

I don't approve, and I'm writing to say so ; not that I expect that to make any difference. I think, though, that you might have given way to a mother's whim ; I've always pictured Janet's wedding as an event—something for me to have and remember. But there, I suppose I'm old-fashioned.

Still, there is one thing. I'm coming up with Janet to see her married, even if it is only a civil wedding. And you can't expect to marry the poor girl straight off the train. We'll come up on the Tuesday and stay at a hotel for the night and then you can get married the following day . . . .

Well, having won my point it would have been ungenerous—and bad tactics—not to have conceded her small demand.

I met them at the station and took them to the same hotel as before.

I could see that the old lady was still a little piqued with me and I set myself to win her over until eventually I noticed a perceptible softening in her attitude . . . "I told Janet you were a strong-willed young man," she said. "And you are."

"Well, it's better for her to find it out now," I retorted. "Then, at least, she can't say she wasn't warned."

"Still, I dare say it'll stand you in good stead in

some ways. I think maybe you'll go quite far one day if you give your mind to it."

I was genuinely pleased at this expression of her belief in my ability and I told her that we'd be going to see her as soon as we could manage it.

She and Janet wanted to see the apartment but I told them they must curb their impatience until the next day, after we were married. It was to be a surprise for Janet.

" But then I'll not be seeing it at all. You'll be going straight off on your honeymoon."

" I'm afraid," I said, " that we'll have to postpone our honeymoon for a while."

There was a silence then and I knew they were both staring at me. " It's not very romantic, I'm afraid," I went on. " But this is a difficult period for the business and we can make up for it later on."

The old lady snorted. " First, no proper wedding and now no honeymoon. I must say you have strange ideas, young man. I'm beginning to have my doubts about this marriage. Why, I never heard of such a thing. If you—"

Janet put out a restraining hand. " Don't Mother, please."

" Oh, very well," Mrs. Playfair subsided, grumbling. " But the whole thing seems extraordinary to me."

When I had Janet to myself for a few minutes I took her arm. " Darling, you do understand about the honeymoon? "

" Yes. At least I think I do," she said, hesitatingly. " It is a little disappointing, of course, Dex. I'd been thinking of so many places we might have been going to. But—you know best, dear. If it can't be managed, it can't."

" Well, the truth is that I should have waited a while longer. Then the garage would have been able to stand on its own feet and I would have felt free to leave it for a while. Instead of which I've been so darned impatient to have you with me that I just couldn't wait that long. That's pretty selfish, I expect. Just because I'm so crazy about you isn't sufficient reason to rush you like this—no honeymoon, only a small flat . . ."

She stopped me with a smile and her eyes were alight. " That's rather a compliment really, darling, isn't it—not being able to wait for me? "

" That's the way I feel," I said and held her close and kissed her fiercely.

When I released her, rather breathless, I said : " Anyway, I'll make it up to you later on. We'll have a long trip wherever you want to go and a large house and everything you want to go with it."

" Silly ! " she said fondly. " I don't want a big house or grand things. Just a home, that's all. And wherever we are, that'll be home from now on."

After the simple ceremony the next day, we all went along to the apartment.

" My goodness ! " Mrs. Playfair said on the way. " Is that all there is to it? Why, I hardly feel that you've been married at all."

" Don't worry," I replied, holding Janet's hand and looking at her. " We're married all right and that's the way we're going to stay."

" Well, I should hope so," said Mrs. Playfair.

Janet's ring was winking up at us from its new, rather self-conscious home and we both looked down at it. Then her hand tightened in mine and I pressed back.

I think we both felt rather pleased with ourselves.

To be newly-married! There is no feeling quite comparable to that in the whole world. The absurd, yet lovely sense of exhilaration! The feeling of owning the earth! Hold tight to it, for, though we believe that it will stay with us always, it is but evanescent, and once we lose it we can never experience it again.

When we arrived, Janet hurried, with small sounds of pleasure, from one room to another. Mrs. Playfair, more critical, took her time.

" It's nice, Dex," Janet said.

" Not bad," Mrs. Playfair admitted. " You'll need another room later on, maybe, but it's big enough for the time being."

" I love the kitchen," Janet said. " I'm longing to get at it and try out my cooking on you, Dex."

" Which is a good enough hint to me that I'm out of place in a post-wedding party for two," Mrs. Playfair said, getting up.

" No, mother, it's nothing of the kind."

" Anyway, my train leaves soon and I have to go back to the hotel."

" But of course we're going to see you off."

And so we did. And then once more we made our way to the apartment. It was two floors up. Near the foot of the stairs we encountered Mrs. Hellini. She was the caretaker's wife, a well-meaning but garrulous old woman, fat, blowsy and untidy.

" Oh, good-day, Mr. Price." She grinned cheerfully at me and looked curiously at Janet and I introduced them.

" Oh, really? Mrs. Price, I am so pleased to meet you." She turned to me. " I didn't know you was married."

" We only got married to-day."

" No? You are just married? Well, that's wonderful." She shrieked with laughter and threw her hands up above her head. " I am happy for you both. To be married it is nice. And to be just married, it is better." Her flabby sides were wobbling with her chuckles. " I am wishing you everything that is good. And lots of babies. It is good to have babies. Yes, I know because I had seven. And triplets I had too. To feed them it was like wasps round a honey-pot. Yes, lots of babies I had. My husband say no sooner one out than another pops in." She stood back in mock alarm. " Ah, perhaps I say something I shouldn't! I get carried away by my babies. But it is good to have them."

Janet had my arm and was edging me away.

" Well, we're only just married," I reminded the big woman as I moved away.

" You can never start too early," she called up after us, and I heard her fat laughter billow out again.

I followed Janet in and closed the apartment door and leant against it. " Well, here we are," I said.

" Yes, here we are," she echoed, looking small and somehow forlorn in the centre of the room.

" Alone at last," I said. My conversation did not seem too bright, I thought.

" Yes."

" Darling." I went across to her and put my hands on her shoulders. " What's wrong? "

She wriggled herself away from my hands. " Please don't, Dex. I don't know what it is. I just feel a little lone—lonesome, I suppose. It's silly, I know, but I haven't really been away from home before. And I— I feel a little shy. It's rather frightening to be alone with a strange young man, really alone, I mean, and married. No, don't be offended, Dex ; I know you're not really a stranger. But—can you understand what I mean? And that awful old woman and her babies ! "

" Yes, of course I understand," I told her. " As a matter of fact I feel rather shy myself. And I'm sorry about Mrs. Hellini. She's harmless, really. Quite a kind old soul. She'd be heart-broken if she knew she'd embarrassed you."

" Let's not talk about it just now, Dex," she pleaded.

There was a silence for a while. Then I said brightly : " What would you like to do this evening? "

She went across to the window and stood looking out of it. " You can see quite a lot of the city from here, can't you? Well, I don't know. What would you like to do? Shall I cook my first meal for you? Then you can find out about my cooking before—before it's too late."

Suddenly her shoulders began to quiver and I knew that she was crying. I went up to her quickly.

" Janet, darling. Your nerves are all on edge."

In a minute she stopped crying and I gave her the handkerchief from my breast pocket.

" I am being a fool," she said sniffing. " Please forgive me ; I'll be all right now. I know," she turned to me, " let's go for a drive in your car."

" Sorry," I said, " but this is the car," and I pointed to various pieces of furniture.

" Oh, Dex, what a shame ! It must have been awfully hard for you to give that up."

I smiled at her. " I've got something I wanted even more. And I can always get another car. Anyway, you're not cooking to-day. It'll be time enough for you to start that to-morrow. Let's go out to dinner

and then go to a theatre. Would you like
that? "

She accepted the suggestion gladly. I think she
would have been pleased to do anything to take her
mind off herself and break the nervous tension she had
accumulated.

Janet threw herself into the evening with a determined, almost feverish gaiety. We had a good dinner
and then went on to a music-hall. The comedians
must have loved her because she laughed at even the
unfunny jokes.

When we came out she said : " Dex, can we walk
home? It was so hot and stuffy in there."

" Of course," I said.

She took my arm and we walked slowly, breathing
in the coolness of the night.

She looked up at the stars. " There's the Great
Dipper," she said. " And the Little Dipper. That's
all I know, I'm afraid. I wish I weren't so ignorant.
There are so many things I want to learn about. Do
you, Dex? "

" Plenty," I replied. " But mainly about business.
The other things can wait till I have the time and the
money."

She sighed. " I know so little about even you.
Are you a clever person? "

" Nothing special. But I'm fairly smart. And I'm
ambitious. It's the people with the grit and the
ambition that get there."

" And what happens to the others? "

" They get left by the wayside."

" But maybe they don't mind that. Maybe the
wayside's quite pretty, really."

" Maybe. It's just not what I happen to be aiming at, that's all."

" You don't believe that success is everything, do you? "

" Well, it's enough for me for the time being. You've got to be successful in this world to be anyone that matters. And you've got to get to the top to be able to get the things that matter, comfort and a decent standard of life. It's success or nothing with me, Janet, and it won't be nothing."

After a while she said a little doubtfully : " Well, I hope you're right."

I laughed at her. " You don't have to worry, darling. You leave that and the success part to me. I won't let you down."

When we got back to the apartment we stayed up for a while talking, discovering new things about each other.

At last I said : " It's getting late."

Janet looked at our new, rather ornate clock on the mantelpiece. " Yes, it is."

We both stood up. I loved her a great deal as she stood there, small and hesitant. What odd creatures women were, I reflected, so many obscure emotions and fears chasing each other about inside them. If a woman feels herself enveloped in love she will yield all gladly, but it must be prised from her slowly, for she is quick to take fright, a sensitive creature lost in a sea of emotions.

I kissed her gently and said : " I'll use the spare room to-night. You're nervous and upset and you need a little time to settle down."

She tightened her arms round me. " I feel that you are two different persons. One so determined and business-like and the other one—my one—tender

3

and loving, like this." Her head went up. " Kiss me
again, Dexter," she said softly.

I complied. It was a long kiss. Almost I felt that
she had given herself to me completely in that kiss.

Then she whispered : " I don't feel shy or nervous
any more, Dexter ; not any more . . ."

3

The miniature screen in my mind took weeks and
months and turned them into seconds.

Janet and I made a few friends but nobody of any
special value. Occasionally I took home someone I
thought it might be worth while to cultivate and sometimes Jeff and Marjorie came to spend the evening with us.

I felt rather sorry for the young couple. They were
obviously very much in love yet they never seemed any
nearer to getting married. I tackled Jeff on the subject
once, more out of curiosity than anything else.

He grinned at me in that attractively impudent way
of his. " Why can't a duck swim without water?
No cash, old boy. No cash, no marriage."

" But surely," I said, " you're making enough to get
married on. It's not a colossal amount, I know, but
you ought to get by on it."

" I suppose we could just about manage on it," he
said. " But when a fellow gets married he needs a
bit of hard cash for various things. Like getting a
home for the prospective bride, for instance. Maybe
I ought to be saving but I guess I'm not the saving
kind. And Marjorie hasn't anything. So there it is :
we just run along until something turns up."

I thought it over for a while and then I opened the

subject at the end of the day. " Look here, Jeff, about what we were discussing this morning. It's silly for you to go on like this. Let me lend you some money. Enough for you to get married on. And if you don't like saving, I can take some out of your salary each week to pay back—after a while, when you've settled down, that is."

" Well, that's an idea," he said slowly. " Yes, I'll take you up on that. Thanks a lot. Marjorie'll be pleased. She's fed-up with waiting.

" And by the way," I said, feeling magnanimous, " it's about time you had a rise. After all, the business is doing pretty well." Besides Jeff was a useful worker and I didn't want him to get any ideas about leaving me.

The marriage was arranged to take place as soon as possible and Janet and I were invited to attend.

It was quite a pleasant little wedding and Marjorie looked almost radiant in her white dress. Afterwards there was a small reception at her parents' home. They had very little money, as I knew, and they must have scraped hard to find enough for this event. Or perhaps Jeff had helped them out with some of the money I had lent him.

The few guests sat down to the carefully prepared meal at which I found that I was the guest of honour. This rather pleased me as I admit I felt a little piqued at not having been asked to be best man. After all, I had really made the marriage possible.

Later on, Jeff and Marjorie left on their week's honeymoon and soon afterwards we took our departure.

Janet took my arm. " I do hope they'll be happy. It was rather nice of you to help them out, Dex, and to give Jeff a week off. You know, I was thinking.

Doesn't it seem odd that we couldn't have either a church wedding or a honeymoon but your employee can? "

I looked quickly down at her but her tone had been quite free from any intention to give offence and her expression was innocent. " I'm not complaining," she added hastily when she saw me looking at her. " I've got everything I want—except perhaps a little more of you." She sighed. " I'm afraid I do wish sometimes you weren't so keen on your business and that I saw more of you."

When we were back in the apartment she came and sat on the edge of my chair and gave me that shy half-smile of hers that I had first fallen in love with.

" Dex, I went to the doctor this morning."

I was alarmed. " Why, what's wrong? You didn't tell me anything was the matter. What is it? "

" Don't get excited," she said. " There's nothing wrong. I've just been taking Mrs. Hellini's advice."

" Mrs. Hellini? What's she got to do with it? "

" Don't you remember, when she stopped us at the foot of the stairs, just after we'd seen mother off? "

" You mean you—you— That's wonderful! When? What shall we call him? "

" Him? Why should it be a ' him '? " she laughed.

" Oh—well, of course it could be a girl, I suppose. It might even be both."

" I hope not," she said.

We spent the rest of the evening thinking of possible names to call him, her or them.

After Jeff had returned from his honeymoon I told Janet that I was going to take her for her delayed honeymoon. There wouldn't be much chance of having it after the baby arrived. I begrudged taking

the time from my work but I felt that it would be unfair
to Janet not to have the holiday as I had promised it
to her. We had a good enough time but I was
itching to get back. I was determined somehow to
build that garage into a sound and more than sub-
stantial business and, though it was doubtless foolish,
it seemed that whenever I was away from it I might
be missing good opportunities.

During the weeks that followed I began to look out
for another apartment, a larger one. I didn't tell
Janet, because I wanted it to be a surprise again.
I would buy what new furniture we needed and have
everything moved while she was in the maternity home.
Eventually I found a place that seemed suitable. All
the rooms were larger and there was an extra room as
well. Moreover the district was better. We were
moving up !

I had the same nerve-racking wait when the baby
was due that most husbands experience. I decided,
however, to stay at the garage rather than hang around
helplessly at the hospital. In the hours of waiting
I worked doggedly on but there was perspiration continually on my face and I hardly knew what I was
doing. I suddenly realised how much Janet had come
to mean to me and the thought that anything could
happen to her nearly drove me frantic.

Jeff, passing me, said : " You're doing about as much
good with that car as a frog. Why don't you go and
wait over at the hospital ? It can't be any worse there."

" Go to hell," I snapped at him and he grinned and
moved away.

I kept looking at the telephone, aching to ring the
hospital but realising that it would only be a waste of
time. They had strict injunctions to ring me as soon as

possible and let me have the news. Why the devil didn't they ring? I went over to the phone and then hesitated and went away again. Then once more I went across and after a moment picked up the instrument and asked for the hospital. I could feel the pulse on the left side of my neck beating furiously as I waited. Then a voice answered and, thickly, I made my inquiry.

"Just a minute," the voice said lazily and, after a pause: "No, there's no news yet."

So casual the voice, so unconcerned with all the tragedies and suffering around it! I wiped my forehead and walked slowly back to my work.

Jeff came over. "Quit worrying. Your wife's probably in there having a fine time. Maybe she's playing a hand of cards with the doctor and a couple of nurses. The hard part's for the man, I say."

I scarcely heard him. "Why do people have to have babies? Damn it all, it's not worth it. All this fuss and trouble and pain. It wouldn't be so bad if doctors knew their job a bit better instead of tinkering round with a woman as if she were a car. Cars haven't been here very long but women—"

The sound of the telephone broke into my tirade and I stared balefully at it, thinking that it was probably not the hospital, anyway. Then I dashed towards it and, panting, picked up the receiver.

"Yes, yes. Hullo."

An impersonal female voice, slightly metallic, said: "Is Mr. Dexter Price there, please?"

"Yes, speaking."

"This is the Maternity Home. Just a minute, Mr. Price, I have a message for you." And then, maddeningly, the line went dead.

" Hullo, hullo," I shouted.

The voice came on again. " Here it is. A boy was born to your wife half an hour ago. They are both doing well. Hullo, can you hear me? "

I clutched at my collar and recovered my voice. " Sure I can hear you. You said a boy? That's fine. Can I see her? I'll be right over. Thanks. Good-bye, good-bye."

Grinning broadly I swung round to find Jeff and saw him at my elbow.

" It's a boy," I said. " A boy. His name's Fenton."

" You mean he came with the name? " Jeff asked.

" Don't be a chump. Imagine that ! I'm a father. Take over, Jeff. I'm going to see Janet. This is great ! Why don't you and Marjorie have a kid, Jeff? "

His face fell. " It wouldn't be so good for us. Marjorie's not too strong. As a matter of fact she's sick again right now. It's sort of expensive, being ill. Maybe while you feel so good you could lend me some more money."

The way I felt then he could have borrowed the moon.

4

Jeff came into the office with a roll of paper under his arm.

" Want to look at something? " he asked.

I looked inquiringly at him and he unrolled the paper. It was a blue-print and he spread it out on the desk.

" I've been working on this at home for some time," he told me.

The design was of a car engine and, though I could

see that there were considerable deviations from the usual types of engine used, I could not take in their significance. Jeff began to explain the design to me. " If this works," he said, " it'll be possible to build really cheaply-priced cars. Look at that. And that. The construction's so easy it's almost child's play. It'll save hours of working-time. And the car'll run on about two-thirds the amount of juice they use now."

I studied the print for a while and asked Jeff a few questions. Then I said doubtfully : " Well, it sounds all right, I suppose. But you'd never get anyone to take it up. The big companies would only be cutting their throats if they produced it ; and the petrol concerns would do all they could to kill it."

He looked disappointed. " I thought perhaps you and I could build a model here and see how it went."

I shook my head. " I think we've got plenty to do right now without bothering about that," I said. " Maybe later on—"

" If that's the way you feel !—" He rolled up the print and took it away.

Fenton was turning from an odd, wrinkled little thing into a recognisable baby boy. At first I couldn't take much interest in him. To me he was just a screwed-up little thing that slept, woke up to bawl and eat and then slept again. But gradually he began to take on a personality of his own and some hair grew to cover his baldness and he learnt to laugh. It was that first sound of his laughter, I think, that drew me to him. The first baby chuckle is the sound that winds itself firmly round your heart and ties the knot.

Janet at least was not so lonely now with the baby

to fill her time but now and then I wondered if I was doing the right thing in sticking to the garage. I couldn't see any way of expanding yet, but somehow it had to be done. We were doing quite well, but that was not enough for me. I had to build up something solid for the boy and perhaps for other boys, too. And I wanted more than just an apartment; I wanted a proper home, a house and some ground, a garden . . .

It was on a Sunday morning that Jeff came to see me at the apartment, his face looking pale and drawn.

I looked at him in some surprise. " What's the trouble, Jeff? " I asked.

" It's Marjorie," he said. " She's never been very well as you know. She's been taken bad again, worse than I've ever seen her. I got the doctor in. She wouldn't let me have him before, always said it would pass. Maybe she was frightened of knowing the truth. Anyway, this time I insisted. She—she's got T.B., Dex, and it's—rather late. I've got to get her away at once. I'm afraid I shall have to pull out . . ."

" That's too bad, Jeff. And I shall miss you."

I meant that; it would be hard to replace him with anyone so good.

He was silent and I thought he was thinking about the money he still owed me; there hadn't been much paid back yet. But he was way ahead of me.

" I—I'm in rather a fix. It's about money again. I wouldn't ask you if I wasn't desperate. I haven't any ready money; I told you I'm not the saving kind. I've got nothing except the furniture, and I owe you that already. And some more." He gestured helplessly. " I guess I just don't know what to do."

My brain was working hard. There was only one

thing of his that had any value to me. I had been thinking about it quite a bit lately.

" I'd like to help you out, Jeff. It's rather difficult though, because, as you say, you still owe me quite a lot. There's not much sense in your loading yourself with more and more debts which you may never be able to get rid of. What about cleaning the board? "

" What do you mean? " he asked, puzzled. " I told you I've got nothing."

" You showed me a blue-print some time ago. A new design for an engine. Suppose you let me have that and we'll forget what you owe me? And I'll give you a bit more besides."

His face became set and stubborn. " I'll be damned if I do," he said.

I shrugged my shoulders. " All right. Just as you like. After all, it's only a gamble. I'd probably be throwing money down the drain."

He faced me determinedly for a few moments and then he seemed to collapse. " I'll do it," he said, running his hand wearily through his hair. " I haven't any choice."

" Come and see me to-morrow," I told him, " and we'll settle it all up. I want things done legally so that I have a free hand."

His face gave a twinge ; it could hardly be called a smile. " You've certainly got your head screwed on right," he said. He sounded a little bitter. Unnecessarily so, I thought. One can't have it all ways.

With Jeff's successor I decided to go ahead after all and build a model from the blue-print. Several factors influenced me in this decision. More and more I seemed to be in a rut and I felt I ought to grasp at anything that might pull me out. Furthermore, unless I made some use of the design, the money I had given to Jeff would be a dead loss.

At first we tackled it in odd moments and I spent much of my spare time working on the model. But as it began to assume definite form I gave more and more of my time to it and at last it obsessed me completely. As it grew under our hands we had to make a few minor alterations but on the whole it was amazing to see how cleverly Jeff had, on paper, anticipated the practical working. We used scraps and spares and made old parts into things they were never conceived for. The body-work consisted of pieces gathered together from far and wide and patched together and painted.

And at last it was finished. We stood back looking at it with some awe. It was not an inconsiderable achievement to have built any sort of car in the way we had done ; if this one achieved its expectations it would be an event indeed.

And then I took it on to the road. For the next few days I tested it in every way I could think of and, like a David to its Goliath, that car of bits and pieces stood up to it and smiled. I refused to let myself be convinced too easily but finally I knew that its worth was incontrovertible. Not only would its design considerably simplify production, not only was its fuel consumption far lower than anything of similar size and power, but, in addition, its general performance was superior to any comparable standard model of which I knew.

In my mind's eye I saw the mass production of the car ; I heard the machines thumping, pressing out the steel, grinding, cutting, shaping. . . . That was music indeed ! I saw a mighty factory, men streaming through to work, cars streaming out : not hand painted and patched, but gleaming, shining things, worthy of their name. Their name? Yes, what would that be. Price? No—not catchy enough. Dexter? Mm—no. Then I had it : Pridex ! Yes, the Pridex Car Company Well, now all we lacked was the Company.

I went to the apartment.

" Hullo, darling," Janet said. " My, you're early. Everything all right? "

" Janet," I said. " How would you like to visit your mother . She's only seen the baby once, just after he was born. Don't you think it's time she had another look? "

" Dexter Price," Janet said, cocking her head on one side. " What's going on in your mind? It's not like you to suggest something of that kind all by yourself. What reason have you got for wanting to push Fenton and me out of the way. Come on, out with it," she smiled.

" Oh, I don't want to push you off," I said. " I'm coming with you."

" Honestly? Why, that would be lovely. I'll write to mother straight away and tell her what train we'll be on."

" Wire her," I said. " We're going to-morrow— and we're going by car."

" Well, it was nice of you to bring them to see me, Dex. Though I don't suppose it was your only motive in coming." The small old lady twinkled at me. Janet was upstairs with the baby.

" You're a wicked suspicious old woman," I said.

" Maybe I'm getting to know you. And what's that strange contraption you came down in? "

" That ' strange contraption ' is going to found the

family fortune. Now, can you do something for me? "

" Ah, here it comes ! "

" All I want you to do is to ask Mr. and Mrs. Marsh over for dinner."

" And then? "

" That's all. The rest's my job. I want to manufacture cars and I want Mr. Marsh to do the legal part and find me the financial backing, if possible."

" I see." She took it quite calmly. " Is it a sound proposition? "

" If that car out there's anything to go by, it's more than sound. I could sell it to any of the big companies —even if they only bought it to hide away ; because if this goes on the market they're going to have to fall in line. But this is the way to make something big of it. Of course, it's a bit of a gamble. Anything new is. But I'm willing to risk everything I've got on it."

" Very well, I'll do my part. I have some savings tucked away too. I'll let you have them."

" I'd rather you didn't. If anything happened !—"

" Don't be silly," she said. " If there's anything good going, I want to participate."

I felt grateful to her ; she was showing her trust in me. I hoped that Mr. Marsh would have as much faith.

They left us alone after dinner.

" Nice to see you again, my boy," Mr. Marsh said, clipping a cigar. " And Janet's looking well. We would like to see more of you both, but I suppose you're busy. . . . Janet's mother was most upset that you couldn't be married here. Ah, well ! I understand that you have something to say to me."

I told him about the car and my ideas for its production.

He listened attentively, drawing at his cigar and asking a question now and then.

When I had finished he scratched his ear and smiled. "You're aiming rather high," he said. "Now, look here, suppose that all you say is correct—and I've no doubt that it is since this is your province—don't you think it would be wiser to start in a smaller way? I know it's pleasant to dream of huge concerns but very few that I know have ever started like that. You have to build up to it and prove that you're capable of expansion. You see, most of it would be public money that you'd be risking. Now, my advice is this. First, let's have the design patented. Then we'll get a company formed and I'll try to interest some people I know. And to show my faith I shall invest in it myself. Then we acquire a suitable factory, possibly somewhere where there's room for expansion. The rest is up to you."

I accepted this undoubted wisdom for what it was and immediately began to think of all the splendid things the future was to bring. I was on my way up with a vengeance. Garage proprietor—and soon now Managing Director of a car manufacturing company!

The next few weeks and months were filled with bustle and activity, interviews and meetings. Under my hands and with the kindly guidance of Mr. Marsh I saw my plans slowly materialise. The buildings were prepared, the machinery installed, men engaged. I began to feel like a minor Napoleon of Industry.

Slowly the wheels began to grind and with a hum and a roar the dreams became factual. The cars began to emerge—the sleek, shining models I had seen in my mind's eye. The trade papers reported favourably, the dealers and distributors took to them and, best of all, the public bought them.

" Nothing can stop us now," I said to Janet.

" Dex—" she began, and I could see there was something on her mind.

" What's bothering you? " I asked.

" I was just thinking about Jeff. This car was his idea, wasn't it? I don't know anything about business, dear, but oughtn't he to be your partner or something?"

She was quite earnest. " Listen, honey," I said. " I bought the design outright—all legal and above board. And good business too, as it turns out. But it may not have been so good. I took that risk and all that's built up from it has been my doing. Because of that, no one has any claim on me at all. That's the way things go. All's fair in business, you know? "

" I see," she said, and I thought she looked at me a little curiously. But she didn't mention the matter again.

It was some time later that she showed me a notice in the personal column of one of the papers. It said that Marjorie had died. Probably the notice had been inserted by her parents.

" That's tough ! " I said. I felt sorry for Jeff ; but he must have expected it as he'd told me the disease had been left too long.

" It would be nice if we sent a large wreath," I told Janet. I didn't see what else we could do.

THREE

I

WE stood outside gazing at the house. Janet seemed to have been struck dumb.

At last she said : " It's really ours? Our own house? "

" All ours." It was hard for me to keep a certain amount of pride and self-satisfaction out of my voice.

She put her hand on my arm. " Let's go in ! " she said eagerly.

I had had the house redecorated and everything gleamed newly at us as we went on our tour of inspection. The furniture, too, was new—and expensive.

When we had finished, Janet sighed. " It's nice," she said.

I detected a note of disappointment.

" What's the matter? Don't you like it? " My voice was a little sharp.

" Now don't get cross, Dex. Of course I like it. It—it must have cost you a lot of money."

" Well, what's the matter then? There is something," I insisted.

" Oh, dear, don't make something out of nothing, Dex. It really is very nice. It's only that I shall miss some of our things—our other furniture."

" It's junk," I said, " compared with this."

" And this is all so new and—formal. I shall feel that I'm in someone else's house all the time."

" Don't be silly," I said roughly. Janet was so childish and fanciful sometimes. " This is the very best I could get."

" I know, dear. You always want the best. But— perhaps it's just that I would like to have chosen some of it. At least, the bedroom suite. It's all so—so impersonal. You never ask me about anything. . . Oh, and now you think I'm just ungrateful. And I'm not meaning to be."

"All right," I said, "we'll sell the whole damned lot and you can go round the junk shops and pick up your bits and pieces. I didn't tell you because it was a surprise."

"Wherever we've lived, it's always been as a surprise," Janet said suddenly. "Don't you think a woman has an interest in her own home?"

"I see. So you don't like the house either, and you haven't approved of the apartments we've had! Who do you think I took them for—myself?"

She came up to me. "Please, Dexter. We're both saying things we don't mean. Don't let's go on. I wish I had never said anything. I didn't mean to. I do like the house, really. And when I've changed the things around a bit I shall feel more at home with them."

"I never thought you would want to buy any of the things," I said. "Anyway, I had good advice; in fact, I had an expert buy most of this for me; he arranged the decoration for the house. Besides, you forget, Janet, this isn't only your home; it's also the place where I shall have to bring people to entertain them, business people, and so on. And naturally they must see that I have good stuff."

"I see," she said slowly. "Business is a formidable thing, isn't it?"

"It may be. But's it's the one thing that gives you all the other things you have."

"Not *all*. How odd you are, Dexter. You still hardly know me at all. I want so little out of life and

you want so much.   Or is it that I want too much and
you too little? "

It was useless to argue with her when she was in this
kind of mood and made strange remarks like that.
Occasionally, it had happened before : a hidden and
unsuspected Janet had popped out of her small,
demure frame, soon to vanish again as completely as
she had come.   It would be wise to leave her for a
while and when we met again she would have forgotten
the whole incident.   I looked at my watch and made
some excuse about an appointment I had, leaving her
there to become acquainted with her new home.

It was while we were at breakfast one morning.
Only Janet and I were there because Fenton was being
looked after by Alice.   Alice was our maid.   She was
also cook and nurse : in short, a mother's help.   She
managed Fenton extremely well and made things much
easier for Janet who had discovered that running a
house is quite a different thing from looking after an
apartment.

I was looking through my morning mail.   Janet
poured me out some coffee and said : " I have a surprise for you, dear."

I scarcely heard her because I was so engrossed in
what I was reading.   I looked up at her vaguely and
she repeated her remark.

" Good," I said, still not taking it in properly.
" There's a letter here from Jim Carter.   He says—"

" Jim Carter can wait," Janet said loudly and with
sudden spirit.   " If you remember, I said something
to you first.   I said I had a surprise for you."

Her tone in itself was a surprise.   I realised that she
was having one of her awkward moments.

" All right," I said mildly. " There's no need to get excited about it. What Jim Carter says is important."

" Blast Jim Carter ! "

" Be reasonable, Janet. Just because I don't get excited about some little thing you have to tell me and want to tell you something really important—"

" Little thing is right," she declared, standing up. " And what's more important than your child? "

" Child? What's he been doing? "

" Doing? Why, he hasn't arrived yet. And I'm beginning to wish he weren't going to."

I stared at her for a moment and then stood up and grinned until her face softened and she smiled back at me.

" Sorry, darling," I said contritely. " You were quite right to bawl me out. What's it going to be this time, boy or girl? "

" Suppose you tell me. You were right last time."

" Hm ! All right—it'll be a boy. And then we'll have a girl and another boy. Three boys and a girl : that's a good proportion."

" Here—steady, Mr. Price ! One step at a time, if you don't mind. Since you know it's going to be a boy, what do you want him called? "

In a flash the idea came to me and I liked it the more I thought about it. We'd name him after Joe Marsh. " We'll call him Joe," I said.

I was certainly not prepared for the outburst that this provoked. She turned on me like a tiger cat.

" No," she said. " That's one thing we won't do. Anything but that ! "

Her tone nettled me. " What's wrong with it? I've never seen you like this before, Janet. What does

Joe mean to you after all this time that you can't bear
to have his name used? Am I finding something out at
last—that secretly you still think about him, that even
dead he means more to you than I do, that you wish
you'd never married me?"

She sat down again. She was pale and trembling a
little but her voice was calm.

"How foolish you are sometimes, Dexter. Of course
I still have fond memories of Joe. I shall always have
them. But you who have had so much more out of
life than poor Joe ever had a chance to have, are you
jealous of the few thoughts I spare him, crippled as he
was and dead as he is?"

"I don't understand you, Janet. You always twist
things round to put me in the wrong. Then why are
you making such a fuss about calling a child Joe?
I thought you'd like it if we named one of our sons in
his memory. Joe would have liked it if he'd been
alive."

"If he'd been alive!—" she repeated softly. Then,
wearily: "It's no use. I can't explain it to you.
I hope to God it's a girl, that's all."

She had her way. The child was named Elizabeth.

2

It was a considerable surprise for me when Jeff
came to see me.

"Mr. Jeff Wilson," the girl announced and I had to
think for a minute before I remembered. I had met
so many different people since I had last seen Jeff and,
though I had wondered about him once or twice, my
mind was usually too full of current matters for

abstract speculation about people I was not likely to see again.

The first thing I noticed about him as he came in and we shook hands was that he looked older. He had matured faster than the actual length of time which had elapsed since he had gone away with Marjorie so suddenly and tragically. He had lost his boyish look and seemed to have acquired instead a certain gravity and self-assurance. Only his fair hair was still the same and uncontrolled.

" Well, hullo, Jeff," I said. " I'm glad to see you. Janet and I often wondered what had happened to you. We were very sorry to hear about Marjorie, of course. That was pretty tough."

" Yes," he said. " Well, that was how the cards were stacked."

I motioned him to a chair and offered him a cigar. He refused but took a cigarette.

" Tell me," I asked, " what have you been doing with yourself? "

" Oh—" he gestured vaguely—" I've been around. Here and there, you know. Odd jobs and new faces. I felt I couldn't stay put anywhere very long. You know how it is."

" Sure. You felt a bit lost without Marjorie."

He looked round the office. It was a pleasant room and comfortably furnished.

" I hear you've been pretty successful," he said. " That little design of mine came up to scratch after all. They're good cars ; I've tried them."

" Yes, your idea was fairly sound, Jeff. Of course, there were a few modifications, but on the whole it was a good piece of work."

He seemed a little nervous and I wondered what was

on his mind. His clothes weren't any too new, when I came to think about it, and I wondered if he was in need of money.

" I don't know how things are with you, Jeff, but if a cheque would help . . . For old time's sake."

" No, no," he said. " I didn't come for that. But I wouldn't mind settling down again now and I— wondered if you might be able to give me a job."

A job? Well, why not. . . . After all, he was a good engineer. And when all was said and done, it was his conception that had set us going. Yes, I'd paid for the design and taken the risk and I hadn't any qualms on that score, but still, I could hardly refuse him a job.

Jeff must have misread my hesitation while I was thinking it over, for he took his hat and rose to go. " Never mind ! " he said. " It was only—"

" Sit down, Jeff. I shall be glad to have you working here. I was just thinking how we could best use you."

" Oh !—" he smiled, and sat down again.

" I've got an idea. We've really been concentrating on this one model—except that we also make a larger edition. There's nothing wrong with that : it's paying big dividends. But the car business is always on the move and we ought to be looking out for new things— improvements, variations, new models. Well, that's what you can do, Jeff. You can be our experimental department, look out for the cars of the future. What about it? "

I could see he was pleased. " I'd like that," he said. " Will I have a free hand? "

" Yes. We'll fix you out with a room—and a couple of assistants if you want them. Start in next

week and meantime I'll have a word with the other
directors and we'll fix up your salary."

" Maybe they won't like the idea."

I grinned at him. " I don't ask them ; I tell them.
There's only one boss of this show. And they needn't
worry ; I'm doing all right for them."

I held out my hand. " Come along and have dinner
with us. We live at 16, Parkway now. Janet'll be
glad to see you again."

Business so far had been steady and satisfactory but
suddenly it took a leap upwards. It boomed ; there
is no other word to describe the change, the surge of
orders that flooded us. Everyone, it seemed, had
become car conscious.

" If this keeps up," I told Mr. Marsh and the other
directors, " we'll need new premises."

" Take it easy now, Dexter," Mr. Marsh said, and
the others tried to look profound and duly added their
own words of caution. They were always like that.
They enjoyed making money but they were constantly
afraid to take any new steps, to take the plunge in any
direction. I had always to drag them along with me.
Soon, I reflected, if I was careful and played my hand
properly, I should be able to dispense with most of
them and replace them with a Board of my own choosing. They had served their purpose.

" We can begin thinking about it, anyway," I said.
I knew I would get my own way eventually, as I always
did. But it annoyed me that I had to fight them over
everything I wanted. They thought me young and
impetuous and I thought them static and woolly-
headed. I wanted a Board that was ready to
dare the world with me, that was always looking

ahead, not one that was tethered to a single spot.

It came as rather a shock to find that Janet, too, was opposed to progress. When I told her I was thinking of building a new factory she said much the same as the directors had said.

" You ought to be on the Board, Janet," I laughed. " You must have some cautionary Scottish blood in you somewhere."

" Well, dear, don't forget you haven't been going awfully long. Wouldn't it be wise to see how things go for a few years? "

" A few years? " I echoed. " Months, perhaps. Two years at the most. I admit I'm thinking ahead. But no longer than that. When you say a few years, I expect you mean about ten. By that time, if all goes well, this Company will be one of the largest in the world. That's my aim, anyway."

She came up behind me and put her hands on my shoulders. " Well, if you say you'll do it, Dex, I expect you will. And will you be happy then? "

" It's not a question of happiness," I said, frowning. " One must have an aim in life and whatever one takes on one should try to make a success of. Otherwise I might just as well have stayed at the garage all my life. But where would that have got me? "

" It all depends where you want to go," she murmured.

" Well, I know where I want to go and I'm going there." Sometimes Janet nettled me. I thought she did it deliberately, but I was never sure. I often wondered if she was secretly laughing at me, but I could not see what there was to laugh about so I dismissed the possibility. It seemed to me that only those who had no chance of achieving success laughed at it. Personally, I never had any doubts about it at all. My family, whilst not exactly poor, had had little money to spare, and it was constantly borne in on me that money was the key to many doors in life that were otherwise locked. Money brought power. If one was not to be an under-dog, one must be on top—and that is where I determined to be. And the higher the better.

"Anyway," I said. "There's one thing we don't have to wait for and that's a bigger house. I've got my eye on one that would just suit us, and it's only just come into the market."

The more I see of women the less I find I know about them. How could I foresee that anyone could look askance at the chance to have a fine, lovely home with servants enough to keep the place well run?

Janet came round to face me. She was seriously perturbed. "Dexter, you're not going to move from here? Not after I've dug myself into it and arranged everything as I want it. Why, it—it's part of me, the only house of my own I've ever had."

"You'll soon settle down again. The other house can't be compared with this. It's a lovely, large—"

"But I don't *want* a large house. All I ever wanted was a small house that I could look after. Just a small home of my own, Dex. Oh, won't you ever understand? Everyone's not like you. We don't all want the biggest, most expensive things. Some of us are content just to be comfortable I don't ask very much of life—just a small home of our own and my family round me. I don't want to live in and look after a—a showplace or a suite of public rooms."

"You'll have servants to look after the house for you."

She stamped her foot. " I don't *want* servants."

I stood up. This was an issue that had to be settled once and for all.

" I don't think you're looking at things very clearly, Janet. There are many points to be considered. First of all, there's our family. We've two children already and I hope there are going to be more. But they'll want as much room as we can give them—rooms of their own, rooms to play in, space to entertain their friends when they're older. Then there's my position. I know you don't care about that ; you can't understand how I feel about it. But the fact remains that I'm going up and I expect you to go up with me. As the company expands so will the importance of my position increase with it. But there are things that go with that, things that help me and keep my position secure. I have to meet people, cultivate the right kind of people, make friends with them ; entertain them. Part of that's your job, Janet, though I never thought I would have to tell you so. A woman can help a man a great deal. Surely you're not going to let me down ! "

" So what I want is not important? "

" I don't say that. I only say that I think you're looking at things from the wrong angle. It will just be a different kind of life, that's all. Once you begin, you'll enjoy it. Why, hundreds of women would jump at the chance. A fine house, servants, plenty of money . . . Not to want that wouldn't be logical."

" Women are illogical," Janet said wearily. " All right, Dexter, I give in. You do as you think best. You will, anyway."

" I don't want you to feel grieved about it, Janet. I hope you realise that all I'm doing and trying to do

is really for your sake—yours and the children's. It's
my duty to provide for you in the best way I can.
Even if you don't agree with me now, I think you will
eventually."

Looking round the lofty rooms of our new house, I
thought of how far we had come since our marriage,
and how quickly. We were not using the whole of
the house—not to start with. Yet even so it meant
that I was living right up to my income. I didn't
mind and I had no fear for the future. It seemed to
me that my outlay would be returned with interest.
As I had told Janet, it was necessary for me to get to
know influential people, people with money. Nothing
is truer than that money breeds money and certainly
there were beginning to come into our house men who
represented large sums of that commodity. When I
wanted backing for future schemes, these were the
men who would back me. And so I looked upon their
entertainment as an investment.

Janet had settled down to her new way of life, as I
had known she would and, becoming reconciled to it,
entertained as if she had been born to it. Alice now
looked only after the children and we had also acquired
a cook, a parlourmaid, and a gardener. In due course
we would have, too, a butler and perhaps a house-
keeper. I was doing pretty well, I thought, for such
a young man and I could tell from some of the glances
I received from people I met for the first time that
others thought the same.

And suddenly in my mind there was a flurry and a
pandemonium of scenes, flashes almost ; myself at the
office working furiously, or talking to someone about
a new idea, gesticulating wildly, talking at top speed ;

cars being assembled ; Janet with the children ; dinner parties ; and so on and on until the tempo slowed down again and I was back with my directors once more.

"Gentlemen," I was saying, "some considerable time ago, almost two years in fact, I suggested that if we continued to do well we would require larger premises. Since then we have, as you know, gone steadily from strength to strength. Our potential selling output is obviously much larger than our actual rate of production. It seems, therefore, that we should delay no longer but should proceed on the lines indicated immediately. We haven't room here for the premises I have in mind but I have taken an option on the Klessen site, which would suit us very well. I have here plans which I've had drawn up for the building of our new factory. I don't think you will find much wrong with them. I also have a satisfactory offer for the sale of these premises. I think you will all agree with the steps I've taken and with those I propose to take."

Whether I really thought that, I cannot say, but I was certainly not prepared for the storm of dissension that the proposal eventually provoked.

First they looked glancingly at the plans. But they were not really interested in them, only in what the cost was going to be. It was too much, they said. It would cripple the company. Rudely I told them that they were thinking of themselves, not the company. They were perturbed because it would keep profits down for a while. But eventually they would gain considerably by it.

They protested that they were thinking only of the other shareholders, that it was our duty to protect their interests and not rush wildly into grandiose schemes.

I flared up at that. Grandiose schemes! I told them I'd been thoroughly into everything for weeks.

Why hadn't I consulted them before, then, instead of waiting till the option was due to run out?

I was even more rude then. I told them that their main business in life seemed to be making money. Mine was the running of the factory. When the one was compatible with the other, I did my best to achieve the harmony. With the new premises we should be able to enter the motor car industry in a big way and probably become one of the leading manufacturers. If they didn't want to participate they had an excellent opportunity to retire from the arena. . . .

Slowly, reluctantly, they came round. We went carefully into the plans and the finances of the scheme. And at last they all agreed, as I had known they would.

All the same, I was annoyed when it was all over. The intense opposition which I had had to overcome had antagonised me. Perhaps I should have been elated at my victory. Instead, I was angry at what I considered the obtuseness of my fellow-directors. It seemed to me that they would be a hindrance in anything I undertook. I was too young and impetuous to look on them as a possibly useful brake to impulsiveness.

Mr. Marsh spoke to me afterwards.

" Well, Dexter," he said. " I hope you're doing the right thing. Personally I think it's a great mistake to rush your fences until you're ready for them and that's why I opposed you on this."

" It seems to me, Mr. Marsh, that you're always ready to oppose any suggestion I make, on principle. Perhaps you feel that anything I undertake is bound to be a mistake."

" Oh, come, that's hardly fair, is it? I backed you originally, didn't I, when you came to me with the design for the car? "

" Well, you haven't lost by it. I'm making money for you. And when I suggest making a good deal more, you oppose me. It doesn't make sense to me."

" Perhaps," said Mr. Marsh slowly, considering his words, " it's partly the way you go about it that's to blame. You see, you don't consult any of us before-hand but just go ahead. And then when it's all cut and dried you lay it before us and demand our appro-val. A little—um—dictatorial, don't you think? "

" I'd look pretty foolish," I said hotly, " if I made suggestions that wouldn't bear examination. But when I put anything up to the Board, you can at least be sure it's workable."

Mr. Marsh sighed. " Well, perhaps we're just a lot of old fogies, as I dare say you think we are. But tact is a great thing and probably we all like to feel that we're making some contribution. So if you'd only dis-cuss things with some of us, instead of just going ahead on your own, you'd probably find things a whole lot easier."

I considered him carefully before replying.

" Mr. Marsh," I said at last. " You may think you're acting in the interests of the shareholders. All I'm concerned with are the interests of the factory. I do what I think best and the Board must accept that. I will not waste my time discussing a whole lot of matters with people who know nothing about them and who couldn't help, anyway. I'm sorry we disagree about things, but there it is. I have to go along now : Janet's expecting me. Please give my regards to Mrs. Marsh."

And with that, I hurried off, leaving him gazing after me.

I knew that if I stayed any longer I should simply lose my temper. I was fed-up about the whole thing, the opposition that I had had to wear down, the interminable arguments. . . . Almost I decided to throw up the idea. But no, why should I let my plans go? It would be ridiculous to lose the opportunity out of pique.

I was still fuming as I went to meet Janet in the car. I had promised to call for her at the doctor's where she went for pre-natal attention. Soon, our third child was due to be born. Fenton, the eldest, was five and Elizabeth almost three.

" Good spacing," I had told Janet. " And this time it will be a boy."

Janet was waiting for me.

" What did he say? " I asked as I helped her into the car.

" About two or three weeks."

I grunted and started the car.

Janet stole a look at me. I felt it rather than saw it. " What's the matter, Dex? Something's upset you."

" I'm all right," I said.

" There's something wrong. I can tell. You look all ruffled."

" We had some trouble at the meeting over the new factory."

" The plans? "

" Yes," I said.

Janet looked at me quickly. She knew how I felt about it. " Didn't they approve them? "

I laughed shortly. " Yes, they approved them— eventually. I had to fight them all. And even after it was finished, old man Marsh came up and gave me a lecture on using more tact.   Damned cheek ! "

" I'm sorry," Janet said and touched my arm affectionately.

But I was still fuming inwardly as I recalled the incident.   " Let's go for a spin," I said, thinking that the air might blow my vapours away.

Janet agreed and I turned the car out of the city.

Once we were clear of the built-up areas I began to accelerate.   Janet was silent and I fixed my mind sullenly on my fellow-directors.   I simply couldn't help it.   For months I had suffered under what I considered their lack of co-operation and now, at last, my feelings had crystallised and in my mind I told them, singly and severally, exactly what I thought of them and what they could do with themselves as far as I was concerned.

This was all very well and a useful way of working it out of my system.   But it took some of my attention from the road.   And as my thoughts whirled faster, sympathetically my foot trod harder on the accelerator so that the car kept pace.

Suddenly Janet said : " Don't you think we're going a little too fast, dear? "

" Too fast for what? " I asked.   " I think I know how to drive by this time."   I was quite ready by then to turn my annoyance anywhere, to imagine veiled criticism in every direction.

To show how clever I was, I immediately began to overhaul a car in front.   There was a third car coming towards us from the opposite direction and normally I would not have taken the risk and tried to squeeze through.   It was a risk and I heard Janet draw in her breath sharply, though she did not speak.

I was lucky to get through unscathed and I paid for my stupidity immediately afterwards. My concentration on getting through the narrowing space did not allow for anything extra. Just beyond was a cross-road which I had been unable to see and which in fact I only saw as I plunged sharply in front of the other car. Across this a fourth car was moving, previously hidden from me behind the approaching car. I hit it as it neared the side of the road.

By the time I saw it I simply couldn't stop. I could only swerve madly to one side. It was not sufficient. The final moments before the crash hung suspended in the air and then there was a frightful jarring and twisting and the sky seemed to fall in on us.

One minute there was a violent raucous clamour—and the next there was silence.

Dazed but practically unhurt I staggered out of the car. People clustered round, lifted Janet out. I pushed my way through to her.

She was lying on one side, her eyes closed.

" Janet ! " I said hoarsely, and took her hand.

Her lips were moving and I bent down.

" Dex," she muttered, " Dex, it hurts."

I couldn't see where she meant and wondered desperately where she had been hurt and how serious it was.

" Dex, I think it's started. Take me to—home."

" It's all right, darling," I said. " I'll get you to a doctor. Where does it hurt? "

" Not—that kind of hurt. It's—it's your son, Dex. He can't wait. Like his father—impatient. Maternity home, Dex."

" For Christ's sake ! " I exclaimed and stood up.

To the nearest man I said : " We'll sort this out later.

Could you lend me your car to take my wife back to town? She's going to have a baby."

He took a startled look at me and then at Janet. "You ought to be shot for your driving," he said. "But I'll help you carry her to the car. You can come too but *I'll* drive. I've got a new Pridex and I want to keep it that way."

"If you've got a Pridex, you've got some sense," I said and bent to lift Janet.

As I was climbing in the car a man detached himself from the small crowd. He was a small man and he was limping. "You can't go off like that," he said. "What about me and my car?" He pointed to the car I had hit.

I found a card in my pocket and gave it to him. "Come and see me and we'll fix everything up. I've got to get my wife to hospital. She's going to have a baby."

I was glad to find later that his leg was only bruised.

"Must be drunk," I heard someone say contemptuously as I climbed in.

Janet was moaning a little and was obviously in considerable pain. I was frightened as I looked at her, frightened that something terrible was going to happen.

If the wait for the birth of our first child had been hard, the wait now at the hospital was torture to me. I scarcely knew what I was doing and over and over again I saw the doctor bending over Janet and gravely shaking his head. And then, crisply, he had begun to give instructions and I was pushed out of the room. "If only!—" I muttered to the floor. "If only!—" I raised my eyes to the ceiling. Recriminations were useless but impossible to avoid. How would I ever be able to live with myself if anything happened to Janet because of what I had done ? How could I live without Janet, anyway?

I caught hold of one of the nurses as she came out. " How is she? How's it going? "

She shook me off. She was in a hurry. " We can't tell anything yet. It will take an hour or two. You'd better relax."

An hour or two! How casual that extra possible hour!

I decided to go out. I couldn't stay there any longer cramped up with myself, my own worst enemy.

It was dusk outside. In a half-daze I wandered along. My clothes were still dishevelled, my manner strained and strange. Eyes were fixed wonderingly on me. I must, indeed, have seemed drunk.

I did not know where I was going ; my mind was fixed entirely on other things. When I came to a small church I hesitated and, impulsively slipped inside.

In there it was cool and calm. All things seemed simple, uncomplicated. A single light lit the altar and, to one side, an organist was playing quietly.

My legs directed me to a seat and I sat there listening for a while. And then, unexpectedly, I knelt. There was no hassock and I knelt on the floor and prayed. I was not very good at it because I had not done it for a long time. But all the same I prayed. And it was not for myself I prayed, but, for once, with no thought of myself. I prayed for Janet because she was sweet and kind and because the world had need of people like her.

I have no idea how long it was I stayed there but when I went out it was with a measure of peace. I believed that everything would be all right.

And when the doctor at the hospital nodded briefly to me and said wearily : " She'll do," I nodded back

knowingly. I had been successful again. Even in that.
" And the boy? "

He looked surprised—as if to say: " How do you
know? " Then he said: " Yes, he's all right. A bit
feeble—but he'll manage."

When Janet said the boy's name was Walter, I
accepted it without demur. In the circumstances I had
no desire to reopen the old idea of naming him after
Joe. After what she had been through I felt I had no
right to deny her anything—particularly anything
connected with the child. Though Janet tried to ease
my mind I could never forgive myself for that episode.
One thing was certain: we could never have another
child.

3

It took a year to complete the new factory. And
moving over was a nightmare. But at last we were all
installed and everything working smoothly. The
organisation of the change-over had been difficult and
I was pleased at its successful achievement, for there
was no similarity between the new factory and the old.
For one thing our labour force had been trebled and
the office and executive staff had had to be enlarged
accordingly.

My own office was large and, in the traditional manner, expensively furnished. This was not so much to
satisfy my own vanity as to present a picture of affluence
to important visitors. I always believed in the truth
of the precept which tells one to make a good first
impression.

Nor could my fellow-directors say I had been wrong in my decision that the time was ripe for expansion. Even at the new rate of manufacture our cars were in constant demand. As profits rose so did the directors' faces grow brighter. Nothing I thought, could stop us now. And I was exultant, with some justification, that at my age I had achieved so much. It would have been impossible for my head not to have expanded a little, in sympathy with that other expansion. There would be no limit, I told myself, to what I could do if I wished.

Naturally, the new arrangements meant an enormous amount of extra work for me. Not that I minded that ; I could stand, and even enjoy, any amount of work as long as it led in the right direction. Night after night I returned to the office immediately after dinner was over and sometimes I did not even go home at all until ten or eleven at night.

But the late hours did not exhaust me. On the contrary, the constant stress of work, of keeping my mind alert, exhilarated me. I thrived on it.

The effect of all this on our home life, however, was not so fortunate.

One morning, when Janet said good-bye to me, she added : " Come home early to-night, won't you? and we'll go out somewhere."

" All right," I said, but my mind was already attacking the day's problems.

" Now, don't forget, Dex," she urged me. " It's a rather special day."

" Oh, is it? " I asked vaguely.

" Just our anniversary, dear."

' Really? Many happy returns. Sorry I forgot." I kissed her.

" Don't be late, then. I'll expect you."

On my way to the factory I thought about buying something for Janet. But I hadn't settled on anything by the time I arrived and it was soon pushed out of my head by more urgent matters.

I was kept going all day long, with only a sandwich and a cup of coffee for lunch, and when, at a quarter to six, John Fernal telephoned me and suggested we have dinner together to discuss a matter we had talked about before—the production of civil aircraft—I agreed at once. I told him to give me an hour to finish some work I had on hand and then to pick me up.

My secretary stayed late too. She often did when I had dictation for her and, though the hours were long, she did not lose by it financially.

At a quarter to seven John Fernal arrived and I left with him. Just as I was going the 'phone rang. I was already on my way out and I called to my secretary to tell whoever it was to ring in the morning. I found later that it was Janet. She was dressed and ready to go out and becoming impatient. Unfortunately my secretary could not catch me in time.

We had a long dinner and talk and I did not arrive home till just after ten.

There were two chairs in the hall with a small table between them. Curiously, I saw that some clothes had been deposited on each chair. On one was an evening dress of Janet's and on the other my own evening dress clothes. A note addressed to me lay on the silver card tray. There was just one line :

It was a wonderful anniversary party.

I remembered then and swore at myself. My first reaction was to think up some story, something plausible. But whatever I said would not really excuse me. At the very least I could have telephoned. And I hadn't even remembered a present . . .

I went quietly into the bedroom. A bed-lamp was on but Janet was either asleep or pretending to be. I went over to her.

"Janet!" I said. "Janet!"

She opened her eyes sleepily. "What is it?" she asked. Her voice was not particularly friendly.

"I'm awfully sorry about to-night—"

"It doesn't matter," she said. "Let's not talk about it."

"But I am sorry. Really!"

"It's my own fault. I should have known better than to ask. The only thing that surprises me is that you don't sleep at the office. There's plenty of room, isn't there? You only use your home as a hotel, anyway."

"Now, don't be unreasonable," I said. "I went out with John Fernal to talk something over and I just forgot all about it. We'll make up for it to-morrow, eh?"

"The anniversary's over, Dex. They only come once a year. Didn't you know? And now I'm going to sleep again."

She closed her eyes and snuggled down.

I looked at her there, the dark brown hair and the fair skin, warm and sleepy. But inside she was hurt, I knew. I pictured her waiting for me, dressed and ready and the disappointment when she realised I was definitely not coming back, that I had forgotten, after all.

"Janet," I said, "isn't there anything I can do to show you how sorry I am? Don't be hurt, please."

" Oh, dear ! " She sighed and turned over. " Don't go on about it, Dex. I'm so sleepy. Let's forget the whole thing. Whatever you say now, you'll never change. It's not your fault, I suppose, it's just the way you are. Maybe if you had some aim in life instead of just ambition . . ."

" More of your double-talk," I said, " that means nothing, and you know it. Aim and ambition are the same things and I've got them both. Those are things no one could accuse me of lacking."

" Well, I think you're wrong, Dex. But I won't argue with you. I think aim is direction and ambition is what you want to achieve. Just now your direction is merely towards your ambition and I think you're wrong because the emphasis ought to be on the aim, the direction, the way you live and how it affects other people and not just on the achievement itself. But it's no use my telling you because you'll never believe it until you find it out for yourself."

" Pooh ! " I exclaimed. " Your argument's all topsy-turvy. It's just playing with words again, but really it doesn't mean a thing. When I've got where I'm going—achieved my ambition, in fact—then I can stop to look round and decide on the way I want to live. I'll have plenty of time then. Meanwhile I have to work hard because it's the only method I know of getting there. There's no short cut. That doesn't mean I'm not sorry about to-night because I am. But I do want you to understand about my work."

Janet looked up at me. " You'll never stop," she said. " Because you'll never get to the top."

I opened my mouth indignantly to speak but she went on : " You'll get to where you thought was the top and then you'll find it's moved on. And that's my last word. Good-night." Whereupon she rolled over and closed her eyes determinedly.

"All right," I said. "Like all women you're just unfair and refuse to argue things out logically. But I'm still sorry—and I'm sorry you can't be forgiving about it, too."

She did not move. And with the lingering echo of what I hoped had been a dignified last retort, I crossed the room and began to undress.

The next day I bought her some perfume. She accepted it sweetly but I knew that the occasion was not quite what it should have been.

Gradually things settled down as the new routine became an accomplished fact and even "the new factory" became at last just "the factory."

For a while I was content with this giant which I felt at work under my control. But slowly I became restless again and began to look around me, seeking fresh worlds to conquer. That was how I was made, never content for long but always looking upwards.

The factory, I knew, would not stand a further expansion under existing conditions. But it might be possible to expand in other directions. There was no reason, for instance, why we should concentrate solely on making cars. It was with this thought in mind that my talks with John Fernal were beginning to take on substance.

Fernal was interested in the possibility of making small civilian aircraft on a fairly large scale and I was becoming intrigued with the idea myself. The notion of having my own plane hit at my imagination. And planes were at least in the same sort of category as

cars ; it would not be like starting in a completely new
direction. Fernal had wanted, he said, to start up a
company himself but he realised it would have a much
better send-off and chance of success if it was sponsored
by a sound company already in existence. He had
been a pilot himself in the war and seemed to know all
there was to know about his subject.

He had some excellent designs and he said he had
already made several good contacts with tentative
markets and he thought it could be built into a big
thing, as big as our automobile concern.

I thought about it for a long time and the prospect
offered appealed to me immensely. At last I put it up
to my board of directors.

As I expected, they immediately threw up their
hands in horror.

" Here we go again ! " I told myself wearily.   It was
apparently to be the usual fight—though I had no
doubt about the ultimate result.

The scheme was that we start up a new concern, the
Airdex Company, issue shares to the public to get the
necessary capital but ourselves sponsor the issue so as
to give the public confidence in the project and take
up a proportion of shares in the Pridex name as an
investment for the company.

John Fernal came to the meeting at my request and
after I had outlined the scheme he filled in the details.
He was a little older than I was. Handsome in a
slightly florid way, he had a bluff and hearty manner
and he had the knack of managing to convey the
impression that he knew absolutely what he was talking
about.

Nevertheless, the faces of the directors remained
cold and hostile. They glanced at one another and

showed their disapproval with a slight shake of their
heads. They had opposed me before : I was used to it.
But never with such a steely resolve as this. I had
known before that I could shake them eventually.
This time I sensed that I should never move them.
And feeling this, I became more incensed than usual.
Perhaps it was because I was not on such firm ground
myself ; all in all I knew much less about aeroplanes
than I had ever known about cars.

After a while, Mr. Marsh suggested that now we
had had the advantage of Mr. Fernal's presence and
his helpful explanation of the scheme, perhaps he
would be good enough to withdraw so that we could
discuss the matter with reference to the company's
other commitments.

I could hardly object to that and Fernal obligingly
smiled and went out.

" Well," I said glaring at Mr. Marsh. " What
now? "

" I've heard of this man, Fernal, before," he said.
" He's been trying to raise capital for his scheme for
some time."

" All right. Maybe he has. What does that
prove? "

" Only that he's found no one willing to back him so
far. There must be a reason."

" Perhaps he's been unlucky," I said.

" He seems to have found a willing listener in you,
anyway."

I jumped up. " Oh, now you're suggesting that
he's taken me in, though he couldn't take anyone else
in. I don't like that suggestion very much."

" Easy ! " he said. " I'm only telling you what I
know about him. If the scheme's such a good one,

why hasn't someone else taken it up? There's no difficulty in raising money for sound projects."

"There are a hundred reasons why someone may refuse to put money up and you're a lawyer—you ought to know them all. It may be the wrong time of the year ; the man with the money may have other schemes on hand ; he may disapprove of flying— There may be any one of a number of reasons. But for myself, I like the scheme. It ought to go very well with this factory ; it'll give us double strength in good weather and a second string in bad. Let's leave other people out of this. You've heard the scheme for yourself. What have *you* got against it? "

"The most important thing," Mr. Marsh said, " is that even if the plane is as good as he says, we have no guarantee that we're going to be able to sell enough to make it worth while. People are hardly very air-minded yet."

"That's the kind of talk that kept cars off the roads for so long," I said angrily. "You've been told the prospects and Fernal's mentioned the contacts he's made."

"There's still no guarantee that they would come to anything."

"Oh, for heaven's sake ! " I said. "How many businesses are run on guarantees of sale? Ours certainly isn't for one. If that's the way you're going to talk, we may as well pack up and die."

We argued and argued without getting anywhere. None of them would give way. They were, for once, united in their determination to stand fast and I could find no breach in their opposition. In fact, it was so marked that it seemed almost like a pre-arranged conspiracy to oppose anything I might suggest. When

I said as much the sparks really began to fly.

I told them that they were obviously opposed to any form of progress by the company and reminded them that they had even been reluctant for the new factory to be built.

" We just like to be sure we're doing the right thing before we actually do it," Mr. Marsh said testily. " But in this we're not at all convinced."

" My own view," I said, looking round the table and carefully choosing my words, " is that not one of you has the company's interetss at heart in any way whatsoever."

There was a dead silence during which I could almost hear the rising tide of their indignation.

Mr. Marsh was the first to speak. " I've had enough of this," he said. " I offer my resignation."

One by one the others followed suit. I think they felt that they would teach me a lesson and expected me to beg them to reconsider. But, as they had done exactly what I had hoped they would, I was hardly likely to ask them to withdraw.

" I retract, gentlemen," I announced after the last resignation had been given.

They all looked at me hopefully.

" Yes, I must retract my statement that none of you has the company's interests at heart. By your resignations you show a most exact knowledge of what this company has needed for some time."

And with that, I left them.

The new directors were carefully hand-picked—by me. The original directors had been chosen either because of the influence of their names or the weight of the money they would invest in the company—or a

combination of both.   But we were well enough estab-
lished now to be able to ignore these considerations.
This time I chose men on whose support I thought I
could count in all circumstances.   One or two were
men who were glad to have their names appear on our
directorate.   The advantage was reciprocal as their
names gave a sheen to the list ; they knew nothing of
business and would be content to leave decisions to me.
The others were employees in the firm—Jeff was one
of them—and they, I thought, would be certain to be
loyal to me, as an insurance for their positions if for
nothing else.

I was wrong about one thing though.   I had made a
mistake when I had included Jeff Wilson.   I expected
my scheme to go through now without any trouble,
but he was immediately against it.   He said that he
thought we ought to stick to cars and not branch off
into something we knew nothing about.   Of course,
the weight of numbers told against him, but I liked to
have a unanimous board and I remonstrated with him
afterwards.

" Look here, if you just wanted someone who would
agree with everything you say, you've got the wrong
man for the job."   The heightened colour of his face
showed up strongly against his fair hair.

" Don't be a fool, Jeff.   But you might know that
I'd been thoroughly into the thing before I put it up."

" You didn't seem to convince the last board," he
said.

I could feel my eyes narrowing as I stared at him.
" What are you suggesting? " I asked.

" I'm not suggesting anything."   Suddenly his face
broke into a grin.   " Don't take it to heart.   You
can't have a whole board of directors resigning without

a lot of rumours going round. All the same, I think you'll bite off more than you can chew one day."

He looked at me rather curiously as he said that and I had the fanciful impression that he was completely detached in the way he saw me ; it reminded me of a scientist examining an insect in a bottle and wondering what it would do next, and I didn't like it.

"There's no need for you to worry about that," I said sharply and went out.

The new company was floated without much difficulty. There were, it is true, a few rumours going round of dissension in the sponsoring company, but they died down, and in any case did not reach the general public who formed the bulk of the investors.

As soon as the details were completed we directed our attention to the organisation of the new Airdex factory. I was naturally Chairman of the company and I put Fernal in as Managing Director.

There were, however, difficulties from the first. Fernal did not seem to have any head at all for practical working and he was constantly in my office or on the telephone asking how to overcome some trouble or other. I soon found that I was being forced to devote too much time to the Airdex and too little to the Pridex factory. It was necessary, then, for me to tell Fernal that I could only give him so much of my time and that if he couldn't manage the place better on his own I would have to find someone who could.

He was not too pleased about that and we had quite a little set-to over it. He reminded me that it was he who had introduced the scheme to me and I more forcibly reminded him that without my co-operation it never would have come into being at all.

There was constant trouble among the workers, and I became even more convinced that Fernal was not the right man for his job. If he had had more experience and personality he would have handled them without any difficulty. As it was, the stoppages and set-backs were so numerous that I thought we should never get into production.

However, the prototype appeared at last. It seemed quite a good-looking machine and passed its tests satisfactorily if not spectacularly. Certainly it compared favourably with others in price and performance.

We advertised expensively and a few orders began to drift in, though in nothing like the numbers I had been led to expect. When I tackled Fernal on this he said that people had let him down; nevertheless he seemed confident that there was nothing to worry about. He said the obvious thing to do was to popularise the plane. The public must be made air-conscious and tempted to buy machines of their own. He suggested that we stage a demonstration and advertise it on a large scale.

It is odd how some enterprises simply cannot fail and yet others seem fated for disaster. Airdex must have been one of the latter. As a tribute to the powers of advertising, the demonstration was highly successful and an enormous crowd surged into the field we had taken for the purpose. All went well until halfway through when an Airdex machine went slowly across the sky with a banner streaming out behind it. ' FLY YOUR OWN TROUBLE-FREE AIRDEX ', it said. And suddenly, without any warning, the plane nosed down and began to rush towards the earth.

At first everyone thought it was part of the act but as the plane approached too fast and too close to be anything but out of control, there was a sudden, momentous hush.

And then at full speed the machine tore into the ground.

A simultaneous gasp rose from all sides of the field and then everyone broke into excited speech and movement at once.

And that, more or less, was the end of the Airdex Aviation Company that I had started with such high hopes.

Of course it was not the crash by itself that broke us but that, I believe, was the deciding factor. Even the few orders we had coming in began to reach a standstill. It was impossible to find out what had caused the spectacular failure of the demonstration plane, though everyone had ample theories to advance and we examined every possible cause of defect before building any more.

Nothing came to light to explain the failure of that particular plane but in the checking-up process I came across something even more serious. A whisper floated over to me that Fernal had been buying cheap material for the company and making a profit on the side. At first I discounted the possibility altogether. But when it came to me again from a totally different source I knew I would have to look into it.

The rumour was only too true. The discreet investigation I had made for me left no room for doubt. Fernal had been lining his own pockets with the difference between first-class material and the stuff he had bought. The accident at the demonstration had been caused by something else but that was only a matter of luck ; any day now we might be getting reports of disasters ; of planes breaking up.

I sat down in my chair—*flopped* is the more accurate word—and wondered what I ought to do. And the more I thought the plainer certain things became. My first reaction was quite obvious ; I was thirsting for Fernal's blood. The second was just as evident. Whatever happened, the company was in for the severest financial handling possible. In deciding what action to take I must visualise which course would do the least damage. If Fernal was charged with the evidence and put through the Courts, it was likely not only that the Airdex company would collapse, but also that the taint would smear itself destructively across the Pridex company. But the cost of replacing the shoddy materials was too high to be undertaken and we certainly could not proceed with the manufacture of any more planes from the materials we had—not now that I knew about it. Even setting aside all moral considerations, the risk of future legal—perhaps criminal—action was too great. If the company just folded up and went into liquidation, the car company would also totter, perhaps, but it would probably keep its feet. Fernal must go free, then. I hated to make that decision but there was no other way.

And besides all this I quite suddenly perceived a truth that had been sneaking towards me for some time. The world was not yet ready for civil aviation on the scale I had planned. It was what Mr. Marsh and his fellow-directors had known all along.

I tackled Fernal as soon as I could.

" Fernal," I said, ignoring his greeting. " You're a rat. You've been cheating the company right and left. That's probably all you ever intended to do, all your interest in it ever was."

His face was white. " Names," he said, " mean nothing."

I knew then that he did not intend to deny what I had said.

" It's a serious charge," he went on.

I waved the report I had received at him. " Don't be a fool. You might realise I've got plenty of evidence."

" I see," he said. He was quite calm. " And may I ask what you propose to do? "

" You owe the company a lot of money. Or there's a criminal charge if you prefer it."

" Money," he said and smiled. " Well, you know what money is. Here to-day and gone to-morrow." He waved his arms vaguely. " But I don't think you're going to bring any charge against me."

" What makes you think that ? " I asked watching him closely.

" Just an idea I have. I've observed you, you know. Think of all the things that might happen. You'd certainly be involved; remember how you fought your directors to push me in? "

" It was the idea I wanted, not you."

" Of course, of course. *We* understand. But will anyone else? There might even have been a conspiracy between us. I'd say anything if I had to . . ."

I flushed and moved menacingly towards him. He backed away, holding his hands before him. " Violence won't help you, my friend."

I paused. " I've already made up my mind," I said, " about what course of action to take. And your cheap threats have nothing to do with my decision which is taken solely in the interests of the holding company. To-morrow you will become ill—very ill— and you'll stay away. Your condition will rapidly become worse and you'll have to go away. You'll have to resign and go to Europe. I don't care how you do it—but you're going to do it and I'll clear up the mess as well as I can after you've gone. And if you haven't started on it by to-morrow—you'll be in gaol by to-morrow night. That I promise you."

He shrugged. " Why not? " he said. " It's a good idea."

" Just one other thing," I told him. " Don't ever come back. And don't ever get any ideas about me again. Because if you do, I might be able to arrange that crash at the demonstration as a charge of murder."

He was really alarmed then. " You couldn't do that. The crash was due to something quite different . . ."

At the door I said: " I'm just as good as you at arranging things when necessary. I won't be seeing you again."

The dissolution of the Airdex company caused a considerable flutter. We framed phrases for public consumption, things like: " History is not yet ready for the private aeroplane " and tried to soften the effect as much as possible. The shareholders lost most of their money and the effect on the parent company was, as I had expected, serious. Yet though the car factory rocked a good deal it did not fall, and so I achieved my object in letting Fernal get away.

It was a bad year for us and we had to lay off a lot of labour for a while. I thought that Mr. Marsh and his friends would be laughing themselves silly over it. But the episode was not without point and I had learnt much from it. It would not happen to me again.

And I determined that the set-back in my own personal progress chart was merely temporary . . .

FOUR

THE next few months were difficult—but not killing.
One could always work to make up what one had lost
and that I always considered the most wonderful thing
about business. With ability, work and experience,
one could achieve anything. Luck was necessary to
start with, but after that there seemed to be no limita-
tions. Not everyone, of course, can stand so much
work. Nor perhaps feel that it is worth it—though
I had no doubts about that myself.

Janet I hardly saw at all. Nor the children. If I
had neglected them before they must have felt almost
strangers to me now. When I had time to think about
it I knew that my attitude must be wrong and sometimes, guiltily, I took home presents for them all and
felt ashamed at the enthusiasm with which they were
usually received.

Yet on one occasion at least the enthusiasm was not
forthcoming. For Fenton's eighth birthday I had
promised to take him to the Zoo. It was a long-standing
appointment between us and the promise had been
badgered out of me by long and persevering assault.
But on the actual day something else turned up, an
important matter needing immediate attention. I had
no choice. Useless, though, to try to explain to a
child the meaning of urgent business. To him there
was nothing in the world so important as his birthday
and his visit to the Zoo with me.

When I told him he looked unbelievingly at me.
" But you promised," he said. " You said you'd
take me."

" Yes, I know," I replied. " But I've told you I just can't take you. Not to-day. What about another day? "

The child just stared at me, his lip quivering slightly.

Janet said : " His birthday's to-day, not another day. You ought to know by now that all days aren't the same."

" They are to me," I told her.

" Then I'm sorry for you, Dex."

While I was glaring at her, Fenton said : " Aren't we going? To the Zoo? "

" Look, Fenton," I said impatiently, " something has come up, something important, something that will help to make it possible for you to go to lots of zoos later on. I'm really sorry, but I'll take you another time."

An idea struck me. " Why don't you take him? " I said to Janet.

Fenton said slowly : " It's not the same thing. We often go together. But I was going with *you*." Unreasonably he added : " It's my birthday."

I shrugged my shoulder helplessly and went out.

Irritatingly, the incident kept recurring to me during the day and eventually I decided to buy him something to make up for his disappointment. I sent someone out to buy an air-pistol. I knew he wanted one. Janet had bought him a birthday present from us both, but this would be a special one from me.

When the parcel lay on my desk I felt happier.

I gave it to him that evening. " Have a look," I said. " It's something you wanted."

He undid the string and took off the brown paper. Then he opened the box and looked in. For a moment

I thought I saw his eyes light up, but his face was expressionless when he looked at me.

"Thank you, Father," he said quite unemotionally.

I was taken aback. I had expected some excitement or enthusiasm. But his face never altered, he was entirely self-possessed.

"Um—you could try it out to-morrow," I said brightly.

"Yes, Father," he said.

After that I gave it up ; there was nothing more to say. Nor did I ever see him use the pistol, though he must often have longed to do so.

Soon after that Janet suggested that she might as well take the children for a holiday to her mother's for a few weeks. Fenton was, of course, going to school now but it was during his summer vacation. She didn't think, she said, that it would matter much to me as I was so rarely at home, anyway. I thought it was an excellent idea and told her so.

A week or so after they had gone I began to feel lonely. The comprehension of what I was feeling surprised me for I had not consciously missed Janet and the children. It was the first time she had been completely away from me for more than a day or two, but I had been working so hard that I had felt I needed scarcely anything in the way of companionship.

Still, even though I must have taken Janet's presence a great deal for granted in the last few months, I undoubtedly began to miss her when she was no longer there at all.

I found myself quite irritable and moody, first in the evenings when I arrived home and was faced with a solitary meal and then through the day as well after a lonely and unnaturally quiet breakfast.

One evening I rebelled. I was home earlier than usual and as soon as I arrived the empty feeling of the house began to prey on my nerves. There was a letter waiting from Janet which served only to emphasise the desolate feeling I had because she was not there to greet me. I decided to go out for dinner and to put on evening dress and pretend to some semblance of enjoyment in my outing.

While I dressed I thought over some places where I might go and finally settled on a new place that had been recommended to me recently and where there would be some music and dancing that I could listen to and watch. I had been told that it was popular, so I rang up and ordered a table. The voice at the other end sounded surprised when I said it was only for one ; no doubt people usually went there in pairs or a party. Well, I would have a party on my own.

The band was playing when I arrived and the sound of its brassy cheerfulness and the general air of gaiety, with the chatter and laughter, and lights and white tablecloths, made me feel better immediately.

The head waiter led me to a table and then paused, dismayed. There were two people sitting at the table that had apparently been reserved for me. He looked at the card in his hand and frowned.

Then he turned to me, his face creased as though he was going to cry at any moment. "There is a mistake. I do not understand—your table has been taken."

He looked so upset and bewildered that I felt sorry for him. Obviously he couldn't turn out the couple already there who were in the middle of their dinner.

"Never mind," I said a little impatiently. "It's not a tragedy. I don't mind which table I have."

His shoulders shot up and he spread out his hands, palms upwards. " But there is not another table, not a single one."

" It's absurd ! " I said. "*You must be able to find me something. I booked, you know."

" This is terrible ! " he announced, looking tragically heavenwards. " I will see what I can do."

And, muttering to himself, he left me standing there. I was getting slightly annoyed. I was also hungry. And my evening looked like becoming a fiasco.

Suddenly I turned and Jeff Wilson and I noticed each other at the same time. He was sitting at a nearby table with a girl. I just glanced at her for a moment and noticed how dark her hair was in contrast to Jeff's fairness, and caught a fleeting impression that she seemed rather attractive and then Jeff spoke to me and I crossed the small distance between us.

" Hullo," he said. " A surprise to find you outside the office. I thought you lived there. Are you waiting for Janet? "

" No. She's away with the children. I got bored with myself and thought I'd get away for a change. And now the fool of a waiter's let someone else have my table and says there isn't another. I believe he's gone to make one."

" Well, that's rather tough," he said. Then he glanced at the girl. " Perhaps—" He looked back at me. " I wonder if you'd care to join us? " He nodded towards his companion. " May I introduce Miss Merlin. Fay—this is Mr. Dexter Price."

" Hullo," she said, smiling at me. " Yes, please do join us." Her voice had somehow a quality of lightness that seemed to linger in the air after she had spoken.

" Well, that's very nice of you," I hesitated a

moment not liking to break up a tête-à-tête. Then I saw their food and felt hungry again and anyway I'd been feeling lonely. . . . I took a spare chair from another table and sat down.

The little head waiter was bustling along, and I waved him away.

" Mr. Price is my chief," Jeff said to the girl.

" Oh, Jeff and I run the place between us," I laughed.

A waiter came over and I ordered my dinner. Jeff and the girl were talking together and I had an opportunity to look at her more closely. Her colouring was her most distinctive feature. Her skin was pale, almost creamy, and this enhanced the darkness of her hair, and the colour of her lips. Her eyes were large and unusual, the whites being of the blue-white colour a small child often has and the irises were a smoky grey, lightly flecked with brown.

She saw me looking at her and I said : " You don't live here, do you, Miss Merlin? "

" No," she smiled. " I come from the same small town as Jeff. I'm only on a visit here, staying at the Central."

" Why, Jeff," I said. " You haven't told me about this small town. It must be quite a remarkable place if it produces people like Miss Merlin. Or is she an exception? The name Merlin has something to do with wizardry, hasn't it? "

" Oh, she's something special," he said, grinning at her. " She used to be a small freckled creature with long spindly legs and then one day I went home after I'd been away a long time and this is what I found. Maybe there was some sort of wizardry, at that ! "

" Stop kidding, Jeff," she exclaimed. " You know

you still see me more or less as an untidy little school-girl."

His face became serious. " I thought I'd made it quite clear that just the opposite's true. I tried to."

Apparently there was something between them, though I did not know then what it was.

" Don't be absurd, Jeff," she said lightly.

I was certain she did not mean the word unkindly but I could see that he stiffened.

" I beg your pardon," he remarked. " I didn't intend to be absurd."

" Don't ! " she said pleadingly. Then, changing the subject : " I should like to dance."

But Jeff refused to be mollified. " Why don't you dance with Mr. Price? And he probably won't bother you with absurdities."

" Jeff, really !—You are—" She bit her lip. " I'm quite sure Mr. Price doesn't want to dance."

" I should like to," I broke in hastily. " Very much."

And indeed I did want to. She was beginning to intrigue me.

She smiled up at me and then made a small moue at Jeff. He had a sulky expression on his face as she glided lightly into my arms and we set off round the floor.

" He seems to be put out about something," I said.

" Oh, sometimes he's just like a boy." There was a note of exasperation in her voice.

" I think you're breaking his heart," I said jocularly.

" Now you're laughing at me. It's all so silly, really. I m very fond of Jeff. We're very fond of each other. But now he wants to make it into something more—and I won't let him. It took me by surprise ; I've never

thought of him in that way—and I'd no idea that . . .
But I don't think he does, really ; it's just because he
hasn't seen me for a long time. Do you think, Mr.
Price, that one ought to marry someone one's known
all one's life? "

" There's no rule against it, as far as I know."

" But it would seem so—so *ordinary*, somehow."

" I'm not going to advise you about your pre-
matrimonial problems," I told her. " Anyway, it's
really no problem at all.   If someone wants to marry a
person sufficiently, one goes ahead. If not—not.
It's the same with anything. If you want something
enough you'll go after it till you get it. Otherwise it's
not worth bothering about. Particularly in marriage ;
it's no good being half-hearted about that."

" I see.   Big business methods ! But I expect you're
right."

We danced in silence for a while. Then I said :
" I'm glad you were here to-night. I feel better
already. The sight of you would lift anyone's depres-
sion."

" What were you depressed about? "

" Oh, nothing in particular. Too much work
probably. And too much quiet at home suddenly."

" Caused by?—"

" Absence of wife and family."

" Oh dear, you're married ! " she exclaimed in mock
anguish. " All the most eligible men are married."

" There's still Jeff," I said.

" Yes," she agreed. " There's still Jeff."

The music stopped and we went back to the table.

Jeff was still looking despondent.

" Cheer up ! " I said. " What you need is something to drink. Let's enjoy ourselves. This is a special

occasion." That was a significant remark in relation to the way I subconsciously felt, if anyone had realised the fact.

The girl applied herself skilfully to bringing Jeff out of his mood and soon we were all merrily enjoying ourselves as I had suggested. When we finally parted company it was quite late and I walked home singing to myself. It is surprising what an evening out can accomplish.

The next day I found myself thinking of Fay Merlin. In fact I woke with her image on my mind and I lay awake for a few minutes consciously thinking about her, remembering the creaminess of her skin and her large, unusual eyes. And during the day I again encountered her image, coming between my mind and my work. I remembered the touch of her as we danced and the graceful sway of her body.

And as I caught myself at it I shook my head and ordered myself not to be a fool. Whatever I was beginning to feel was only because Janet was away. So I told myself and tried to dismiss the girl from my mind. But she was not so easily put off and in the afternoon I made an excuse to myself to give me the opportunity of going down town in the direction of the Central Hotel. All the way there I told myself that I was certainly not going in the hope of seeing her, that in any case it was ridiculous to think I might see her and that even if by any chance I did I would say no more than good-afternoon to her.

And, of course, I found her, though it meant my going right into the hotel and asking for her. By that time my admonitory voice had given up the unequal struggle. They telephoned to her room for me and she came down. I had half expected—and half hoped

—my mental image of her to have been exaggeratedly good but she lived up to it easily. She looked delightful.

She came towards me. " An unexpected pleasure," she said, smiling. " And perhaps an honour too, because from what Jeff said I thought you never had time for social calls."

" Well, I had to be down this way on business and I thought I might call and ask how you were after our rather late night." I did not add that any businesss I had near there was incidental to her, not she to the business.

" I feel very well," she said. " I hope you didn't have any ill-effects. After all, it's easier for me ; I don't have to get up early and go out to work."

" It did me a lot of good," I told her. We sat down and talked a little but I wasn't really following the conversation as well as I should. I was too conscious of her physical presence. It was quite a frightening experience. I wanted to stretch out the short distance that separated us and touch her. I wanted it badly. As I thought about it, it became a sort of panic of the flesh ; I was afraid my hand might move out involuntarily. I clenched it tightly by my side. And when I watched her lips moving, it was not with regard to what she was saying but with a wonder at what it would be like to kiss them.

And each time I became aware of what I was thinking, I resolutely thrust the thought away from me, only to wander after it a moment later.

At last it was obvious that I could not stay any longer, not if I was to keep up the appearance of being a busy man who had just dropped in for a moment or two.

I glanced unseeingly at my watch.

" What is the time? " she asked.

" Er !—Oh !—" I had to look at it again, feeling myself blushing like a schoolboy as I did so. I told her the time and added : " I really must be off now," hoping she would say something to detain me.

But she rose with me. " How long are you staying?" I asked. " Perhaps we'll meet again."

" Yes, I hope so. I shall be here a week or two, I expect. I have some relations here, you know. I don't stay with them, though, because they haven't room. Not that I mind, because it gives me more freedom."

" I suppose you wouldn't—" I began hesitatingly. " No, I really shouldn't ask."

" What is it? " she inquired gently.

" Well, it was just that I wondered if you'd care to have dinner with me one evening. But I'm sure you're quite booked up with your relations and—um—Jeff."

" I'd like to very much," she said. " As a matter of fact I don't see such an awful lot of Jeff."

" Good. That'll be fine. What about to-night? Or are you busy? "

" I'm afraid I couldn't manage to-night."

I tried not to seem disappointed.

" But I could to-morrow," she went on. " Or wouldn't that be convenient? "

" No, to-morrow's all right," I tried to sound casual. " I'll call for you. About seven."

I left her, feeling ridiculously excited.

That evening I thought about her again. One moment I felt elated at the thought of seeing her the following day and the next instant I was upbraiding myself for having asked her. What did I expect from

it? God alone knew! Certainly I didn't ; my thoughts
were far too muddled.

I wondered if she was seeing Jeff that evening and if
so what they would be saying about me. I took out a
photograph I had of Janet and gazed at it. And almost
I decided to phone up the girl and put her off. Nothing
but disaster could come of any association between us.
I saw that quite clearly. And if nothing was to happen
between us, then why prolong the interlude, why make
it harder for myself to keep aloof ? Obviously I was
playing with fire ; I did not deceive myself on that
score. I stretched out my hand for the telephone but
even with it in my grasp my thoughts were battling
furiously—more emotions than actual thoughts . . .
I must, I must, I can't help myself . . . don't be a
fool, don't risk anything between you and Janet : it's
not worth it . . . I must : events will have to look
after themselves . . . It was no use. I gave it up and
refused to let myself think about it any more. If there
was any issue I refused to face it. Coward-like, I told
myself that all would be well : I was creating something
out of nothing. I picked up a book and settled down
to read.

But it was a long time before I went to sleep that
night because my imagination *genie* went and fetched
Fay to me and she was mine and I could not help
myself. And between desire and frustration I had a
restless, sleepless night, waking tired and heavy in the
morning.

I told myself sternly that the whole thing was stupid
and had got to stop. At least I could resolve to be
free of her in the daytime and keep my resolve. And
so I did, concentrating grimly on my work until the
evening . . . And then I hurried home—like a young

lover on his first assignation—to change and see that everything was ready.

Would the servants talk, I wondered? But I was careless of that. I wanted her to myself that evening and that was all that mattered.

When I went to fetch her she was ready for me, looking delightfully young and cool and virginal—yet at the same time warm and desirable. The coolness was in the slim grace of her body ; the warmth was in her eyes.

" Hullo, Fay," I greeted her. " Do you mind my calling you that? "

" No," she said. She seemed amused.

" Where are we going? " she asked, when we were in the car.

" I was going to take you home. I ordered dinner for you—a rather special dinner. But if you'd rather go out, please say so."

" Not at all," she smiled. " Though I don't know that I ought to visit you unchaperoned. But I'll risk it."

" I won't eat you," I said. " Did you go dancing again last night? "

" No. Just a duty call to my relations. Pleasant, but unexciting." So Jeff didn't know she was going to see me ! I was glad for some unknown reason.

" Do you like excitement? "

" Sometimes," she said non-committally.

The dinner, as I had told her, was a special one and I was glad to see that she enjoyed it.

" You're right," I said, when the maid was out of the room. " I should have invited a third person. I might have asked Jeff, of course, but I confess I wanted you to myself."

5

"What will your wife say if she hears about it from the servants?"

I shrugged my shoulders. "What is there to say? Why should one automatically think the worst? I don't think Janet will do that."

We went into the lounge and coffee was brought in.

"Shall I pour?" she asked.

"Please do."

I sat opposite her. I did not trust myself to sit beside her. Already idiotic thoughts were crowding my brain.

She sighed. "That was a heavenly dinner."

"What would you like to do now. Would you care to go dancing . . . or for a drive?" . . .

"I don't know. I'm very comfortable for the moment. What do you think?"

"I'd rather stay and talk to you," I said. "But I don't want you to be bored."

She smiled again. "Of course I won't be."

"Do you play?" I asked, glancing at the grand piano.

"A little. Do you want me to perform?" Her manner was entirely ingenuous and quite free from artificiality.

"Very much."

She rose. "You may not be so eager when you hear me." On the way she stopped at a portrait I had had painted of Janet.

"Your wife?"

When I nodded: "Nice!" she said, and I could tell that she meant it.

She began to play a Chopin Nocturne, and I leaned back and watched her. Those smoky eyes of her were dreaming of things far away and her parted lips, as

she seemed to smile secretly to herself, showed a gleam
of white from her teeth that accentuated the creamy
pallor of her skin. I wanted to go across to her but
I made myself sit there, fighting down the urge.

The maid came in and took away the coffee tray.
As she closed the door behind her I stood up involuntarily and walked slowly across to the piano. I felt
myself trembling a little and breathing faster than
usual. Inside me there was an extraordinary tense-
ness.

I came up behind her. I didn't know whether she
had seen me move across or not but I thought somehow
that she was aware of me. I was right, because she
spoke softly.

" Do you like Chopin? "

" I like you to play," I murmured.

" That's not the same thing."

" I'm not very musical, I'm afraid. I like it when
there's a lilt in it. That's my idea of music. Janet's
a Chopin worshipper."

She was silent, then concentrating on her playing.
Her neck and shoulders were creamy too, I thought.
Was all of her like that? I had a tremendous desire to
touch the soft skin. Oh, God. I thought. What am
I to do? What will she do if I touch her. Will she
mind . . . will she scream? And what shall I do?
And if I don't touch her? . . . My hands were twitch-
ing. Without realising it I found them poised lightly
on her shoulders. My heart seemed to pause ; then
it took on a new acceleration from the contact.

Her playing faltered for an instant and I quite
expected her to stop and turn round angrily. But she
went on again.

" Fay," I said, and my voice sounded harsh and dry.

Involuntarily my fingers began to stroke her with tiny movements.

" Yes? " she answered softly, her voice just audible through the piano notes.

Then I bent down and kissed her neck. She gave a gasp and her fingers stopped half-way through a bar. She swung the top half of her body round. Her eyes were large and startled and for a long moment stared into mine. And then slowly I bent and kissed her mouth, that red, sweet mouth that had tantalised me each time I had seen her. It was soft and warm. It yielded and responded. I experienced a surge of ecstasy and relief. Whatever it was in me that had driven me on had won ; I could not fight any longer. The waters closed over my head and I was drowning, but drowning in a welter of enjoyment like a drunkard sinking in a sea of whisky.

I came up for air and our eyes fastened steadily on each other, my arms still partly round her.

" Oh, Dexter," she said weakly. " Why did you do it? "

" I've been fighting to keep my hands off you ever since I first saw you. Are you angry? "

" I ought to be. But how can I be when I wanted you to? But it's so—so useless."

" Why? " I asked, caressing her face.

" Why—when there's Janet and your children? I'm afraid I can't compete with them ; I haven't the capacity."

I kissed her again. At first she was stiff and seeking escape ; then she yielded.

Breathlessly she said : " The maid might come in."

" She won't. Fay—Fay, I want you."

The startled expression, like a cornered doe, returned

to her eyes. She shook her head. " No, no, I couldn't."

" Why? " I whispered.

" I just couldn't. Oh, Dexter if only—! "

" What? "

" If only you weren't married! Oh, I wish this hadn't happened. Why did it have to be like this? "

I stroked her arms and her neck. I kissed her again and again until at last she pushed me away desperately.

" No, don't Dexter—Please! It's not fair to either of us."

" It's not doing any harm," I said rather sulkily. " Don't you like it? "

" That's the trouble. I do—too much."

" Then why? " I said eagerly. " Fay, you must! "

" No," she stood up. " It's impossible."

I persisted, but she was adamant.

" I think I'd better go," she said. She was even paler than usual and her large eyes had a look of distress.

" You're sorry you came," I accused her.

" I'm not. Of course I'm not, Dexter. We can't help our feelings. It's as much my fault as yours—and I wanted you to make love to me. I love you: I can't help it. Even though I hardly know you. But there's something in me stronger than that. That's why I couldn't—you do see, don't you? If it could have been otherwise!—Good-night, Dexter."

" Won't I see you again? "

" It would be wiser not to, wouldn't it? I don't like being wise, but there it is."

" All right. I give in. But why are you saying good-night? I'll take you back to the hotel."

" No, don't—"

" Of course I will. You'll be quite safe in the car.
I promise you."

She looked at me but said nothing.

We drove in silence, each full of our own thoughts.

I pulled up outside the hotel and we each turned to
look at the other.

" Good-bye," she said gravely, and put her face
forward to be kissed.

" Good-bye," I said, and kissed her hard.

Then she slipped out of the car and vanished into
the hotel.

I drove slowly back, thinking about the evening.
Perhaps it was the best way ! But I began to remember
how it had been when I kissed her and the flame shot
up in me again.

I spent an even worse night than the previous one
and woke up feverish and hollow-eyed. For hours I
had lain and argued with myself. And the only
decision I had come to was that I must have the girl.
Whatever the cost ! I was no longer quite sane about it.

At the office I decided to ring Fay up. I wanted to
be sure no one overheard my call ; I had to be rude
about it. I called in my secretary.

" Miss Miller, I have some important calls to make.
Do you think any of those telephone girls listen
in ? "

She flushed. I don't know why : I wasn't accusing
her of anything. Perhaps she flushed on behalf of her
fellow-workers. " I'm sure they don't Mr. Price."

" How can you be sure ? " I snapped. " I want you
to make sure."

She telephoned down to the supervisor : " Mr. Price
thinks some of his calls may be overheard. What ?
Yes, I know. Well, please tell them, anyway."

She marched out, her back registering her disapproval.

I made a business call first—in case anyone's curiosity had been unnecessarily aroused. Then I rang the Central Hotel and asked for Miss Merlin.

" Hullo," her voice came fluttering over the telephone, driving shafts of fire into me.

" Hullo," I said, and waited.

" Oh, it's you, Dexter ! Good morning."

" Fay, I've got to see you again."

" But we agreed—"

" Yes, I know. But I have to talk to you just once more. Please ! "

" Well, I don't know. What's it about ? "

" Oh, for God's sake ! " I said impatiently. " I can't tell you now. Not over the 'phone."

" Will you promise to be good ? "

" If you want. Will you do it, Fay ? "

" All right then. When ? "

" To-night."

" I can't to-night. I'm seeing Jeff."

" Oh ! Can't you break it ? "

" Not really," she said. " Besides it mightn't be wise."

" Oh, hell ! All right. Don't tell him, will you, Fay ? "

" No, of course not."

" To-morrow then ? "

" Yes."

" It's a long time." It seemed like a vision of years instead of hours. " I'll call for you then. As I did before."

" You promised, you know."

" What—? "

" To be good."

" Yes, yes. I'll be whatever you like. I just want to talk to you. Good-bye—Fay."

" Good-bye, Dexter."

Two whole days to go ! It was like an enormous chasm staring at me. I tore into my work in a fury of activity.

2

I took her out to dinner this time. Over the meal neither of us mentioned what lay between us though I could not help looking hungrily at her from time to time.

At last I said : " I can't talk to you here, Fay. Let's go for a drive."

" All right," she agreed.

I drove about five miles out of town and then stopped the car. I turned towards her though I could hardly see her.

" Fay," I began and my voice was trembling. " I'm going to divorce Janet."

I heard her draw in her breath. " Divorce !— Dexter ! "

My hand felt for her, drew her slowly towards me.

" It's the only way for us, Fay," I said. And then I kissed her hotly, madly.

Her head leaning on my shoulder, she said : " You can't do it, Dexter." But I knew from her tone that she was thinking about it. Suddenly she sat up. " Don't you love Janet? "

I reflected. " I thought so. But I guess not. Not like this, anyway."

I could not contemplate the future, all the things I would have to go through : the scenes with Janet, with others. But at the end of it there'd be Fay—and freedom from this madness again.

"I don't know what to say." She sounded young and frightened. "I never thought anything like this would happen to me. Other people, yes. But not me. It doesn't seem real. To break up a home, a family! It's so selfish."

"It would be wrong not to, now we've found each other."

"You're so strong. You sweep everything away. It's not so easy for me."

"It'll be alright," I said. "We'll do it together. Janet'll take it the right way, I know."

"And the children?"

"I'll provide for them, of course."

She sighed and leaned back again. "I can't fight you, Dexter. You're too strong. Perhaps I don't even want to." She pulled my face down to her.

"It'll take some time," I said after a while. "I mean, to put it all through and to get married, and so on. I suppose . . . Fay, I'm crazy about you, will you come away with me next week-end? Just for a few days while Janet's away. In a way it'll make it easier to tell her, too. It will make it more final."

My hand rested on her thigh and the blood surged upwards and pounded in my ears. "You must come, Fay. I can't wait."

Frightened again, like a young mare in harness for the first time, she jibbed and shied. But by then I was not to be denied, and in the end she consented.

"When shall we go, Dexter?" Her voice was like the fluttering of a bird.

"We'll go on Thursday." It was Tuesday then, but I could not wait till the week-end proper. Till Thursday was bad enough. "We'll go a long way away. Into the country. There's a quiet place I know. I'll arrange everything. Don't worry now; just relax. Everything will work out all right."

I kissed her again and then turned the car and drove back.

"Darling," she said—and I felt that the endearment was her surrender—"I ought to tell Jeff."

"Better let me tell Janet first. I'd hate her to hear it from anyone else. It might get around if you said anything."

She sighed again. "I'll leave it all to you."

Somehow the hours went by and Thursday came. I rang Fay up to tell her when I would call and was reassured by her voice. I had feared she might want to back out.

Later, I went home to pack.

I had almost finished when I heard a car draw up. But I did not think about it consciously. Then I heard some commotion downstairs and voices. I put my head out of the door; I could not see down the stairs but I knew the voices. They were the maid's and Janet's.

The first thought in my mind was one of panic. What had Janet come home for? Had she heard something of Fay? Rumours are quickly born and travel fast. Then I became calmer. That was not likely to be the reason she had come back. It must be something else. But now! Why did it have to be now? I didn't want to explain things to her just yet. Nor have a scene. Besides, Fay would be waiting for me.

Janet came up the stairs and into the room. "Darling!" She came up and kissed me. "Mary told me you were here." She glanced round and saw my packed grip. "Where are you going?" She sounded surprised.

"Oh—just a trip," I mumbled. "A business trip. Something came up suddenly."

"Will you be away long?"

"Only a few days. What brought you back?"

"Oh, I wanted a few things so I thought the best way would be to come and get them. I'm staying the night, of course. I wish you weren't going. Do you have to go to-night, Dex? Can't it wait over till to-morrow?"

"Sorry!" I said. "I must go."

"But surely it wouldn't make any difference! And I'd rather not stay here alone."

"There'll be the servants."

"That's not the same thing. Besides, I thought it would be nice to be by ourselves. Without the children for once. Do put if off, Dex."

"I can't I've told you. I've got to go."

Her eyebrows went up. "All right. You needn't snap my head off. I only asked you—"

"Don't go on!" I said angrily. I was afraid something might happen to stop me if I stayed much longer. "I have to go—so let's leave it at that."

I picked up my case and went to the door. "I'll —I'll ring you when I get back."

I left her standing there. She was staring bewildered after me. I felt badly about it, but I couldn't help myself. I was being torn in two directions—and Fay's was pulling the harder.

Fay lay back in her seat, the dark hair stirred at her

temples by the slight, welcome breeze that rode occasionally through the car. Without the breeze the air was sultry and electric. Fay's pale face had an excited, tense look.

" Happy? " I asked.

She didn't answer immediately, and disturbed, I looked at her and repeated the question.

" Yes, I am, Dexter."

" You don't sound quite sure."

" Oh, darling, I'm happy to be with you. But it's the other things that make me unhappy. I try not to think about them."

" What other things? " But of course, I knew.

" Oh—just our sneaking off like this. I'm not criticising you, darling. Don't think that. But this hole in the corner . . . And your having to get divorced before we can—can get married and go off like this because we belong together."

" You don't have to be married to belong together," I said.

She sighed. " I'm terribly conventional, I'm afraid, Dexter. I just want things to be right. I've always been like that ; I can't help it."

For an instant I was moved by an urge stronger even than my desire. I wanted to turn the car round and go back. And even while I hesitated, my desire took control once more.

Fay was speaking again. " It's not even as if you've quarrelled with Janet. She doesn't know you've changed ; she must be trusting you—"

" I tell you Janet will understand. She wouldn't stand in our way. She wouldn't want to stay married to me if I loved someone else. We can't help these things, Fay."

" I suppose not," she murmured.

Suddenly she said : " It will be all right, won't it, Dexter?   Please promise me everything will be all right.   Then I'll stop worrying."

I smiled at her.   " Of course it will be all right. If we have each other, that will make us strong enough to see things through."

She touched my arm.   " Darling ! " she said, and in that word conveyed all her love and her trust.

"There's going to be a storm later," I said peering up at the sky.

And so there was.   It broke before we arrived at our destination.   The first roar of thunder was close and the jagged flashes of lightning seemed to tear through the air just ahead of us.   The rain lashed down on the car and the wind gathered itself up and pounced . . .

Dinner was ready for us when we arrived—and we for it.   The small hotel was old and mellow and lovely and one felt secure and peaceful there with the storm performing flamboyantly outside.   But we would have to go out in it again, for a minute or two.   This was only the central part of the hotel, with the dining room, lounge and staff quarters.   The living accommodation was provided by individual cabins spread around on either side.

After dinner we sat awhile, talking in low tones and listening to the storm.

" It's a right night all right," said the proprietor of the hotel solemnly as he passed us shaking his head. " Reckon I'd rather be in than out."

I stood up at last.   " Ready? " I asked Fay, looking down at her.

The light reflected softly on her dark hair.   I watched it for an instant, wanting to touch it.   Then she slowly tilted her head up. The large, tender eyes looking up at me, the soft red mouth . . . She smiled and put her hand in mine and I helped her up.

I took the key—our grips had already been sent to our cabin—and we went out into the rain. Our cabin was the third on the right. I took Fay's hand and pulled her. " Hurry ! " I said and we ran, arriving breathless, laughing. I unlocked the door, and we went in.

" Where's the light," Fay whispered.

But I closed the door, dropping my case, and held her there for a moment, my mouth finding hers in the dark and the rain on our faces intermingling.

Afterwards I found the light switch and turned it on. Fay went round investigating. The tiny hall led into the bedroom, and off that was the bathroom.

" Our own miniature house," she said. Her eyes were shining. " My first."

" There'll be plenty more," I said, and held out my arms for her.

3

On Saturday morning I sat in a chair, dressed, watching her as she slept. Uneasily my mind went round and round creating, destroying, searching blindly for a way of escape. I had sensed it the day before ; in the evening my reviving passion had lulled it ; and now I knew it without any doubt. The fever and the madness were gone and I had no more love for this stranger who inhabited my bed. She was splendid and lovely— but I did not love her. When the mist had cleared, Janet was standing there and I knew there was no answer to that. The body of a girl could not take the place of the years we had had together. Mad I had been and blind in my madness, blind to everything but the sudden urgent desire that had possessed me.

It was all over now. I did not even desire her any more. As she lay there she seemed just a lovely girl whom I knew and was fond of. Yet compared with Janet she was a stranger in my life, an intruder even. I knew her physically now. I knew the touch of her under my fingers and I knew what I had once wondered longingly, that all her skin was of the same delightful creamy texture. But it meant nothing to me now : she was a stranger.

And soon I would have to tell her. But how? What was I to say? Obviously we could not go on, with the divorce, with our marriage. Now that I could see clearly I knew it could bring nothing but disaster for us all. And Janet! I had always needed her ; I needed her still. Self-loathing rose in me and grew.

Fay opened her eyes and saw me.

"Hullo, darling. Up—and dressed? Is it late?" She propped herself up on one elbow, her dark hair rumpling about her. Her curving breasts pressed against the night-dress.

I bit my lip. I stood up and turned away from her. How could I say what I had to say?

"What's the matter, darling? Is anything wrong?" Her voice was concerned.

"Fay," I said. "I've got to go back." I turned back to face her.

"But why?" she asked. "We were going to stay till Monday."

My mouth was dry. "This is so difficult, Fay . . . Sometimes words are so inadequate."

I saw alarm spring into her eyes and she sat up. "What is it? What's happened?"

"I've got to be brutal," I said desperately. "If there was something I could do not to hurt you! . . anything . . . I swear I'd do it. You don't know how badly I feel . . . Fay, I can't go on."

She stared at me, those eyes of hers fastened on me as though they were mechanically clamped.

"Can't go on? . . . With—our plans?" . . .

"Yes," I said. I felt better now it was out.

"Dexter, are you saying you can't marry me?" Her voice shook. I could see her breathing hasten and she began to look quite ill.

I took her hand. It lay lifelessly in mine. "Fay, don't get yourself worked up. There's nothing I can say or do. I was mad. I wanted you. I couldn't see any further than that. When I said I'd marry you I meant it. But now . . . I can't help it, Fay .." I began to shout in my desperation to try to make her understand. Her whole body was trembling uncontrollably : she could hardly speak for it.

"It was only a trick to get me to give myself to you. I trusted you. Yet really I knew it all the time. Only I wouldn't listen to myself. I was in love with you." The quivering words spilled out ; they sounded harsh and contemptuous.

"It wasn't a trick," I said wearily. "Or if it was I tricked myself as well as you. I meant every word I said."

"Well, what's happened then? What's made you change like this?"

"Nothing. Except that I've come to my senses. Now that I know the truth I wouldn't be any good for you, Fay. It would be foolish to go on. I hate myself as much as you hate me."

" I don't hate you," she said softly, and lay back on the pillows. " I feel sick. I'd like to die."

" Don't be silly, Fay. It isn't as bad as all that. It's been a shock. Let me get you something."

" No," she said. " Leave me alone now."

" You'll come back with me? "

" No, I'll stay here for a while."

" Listen, Fay," I said urgently. " It's not so bad as you think. Nothing much has happened really. I've loved being with you—"

" You are a fool, Dexter," Her voice was calmer now. " It means so little to you ; how can you understand? You know I wouldn't go away with any-one unless I was going to marry him. I'm just like that. Even then I didn't want to. But to find out the whole thing was a fraud !—Oh, perhaps not an intentional one," she added as I began to protest. " But when I gave myself to you I gave myself in every way. I gave myself because I loved you, because I wanted to live with you—always. And now—" she turned her face away—" now it's all gone ; there's nothing left, not even a shred of self-respect. I've whored myself to your lust and I thought you loved me ! Oh, God, how sick I feel ! "

" Please don't ! " I said, distressed. " Please don't, Fay ! You'll only make yourself feel worse."

I went across the room to a small table and wrote out a cheque for a large amount, a very large amount. I took it over to her.

" Look, Fay. I know nothing I can do can make up for the way I've treated you. But I can help you in other ways. You've told me about your family : they're not terribly well off. This will help them all —and you. People say that money isn't important.

But it is ; terribly important. Don't be proud about it. Anyway, it's yours. It's due to you. It's part of what I promised you—as my wife. It's still yours even if I can't make you my wife."

I stopped, rather affronted. She was laughing, actually laughing. She lay there on the bed and shook with laughter. Perhaps she was hysterical! That seemed to be the most charitable explanation. I put the cheque on the lamp table beside her.

" Aren't you coming, Fay? Won't you change your mind? Or would you prefer to follow on by train later?"

" Oh, for God's sake, go ! " she said. She had stopped laughing.

I picked up my case. I was ashamed to find myself relieved that we would not have the embarrassment of travelling back together. " Good-bye. I—"

There was no response from her. She just lay there staring up at the ceiling. There was nothing more I could say. I went out.

When I got back Janet had gone. I had half hoped, half feared she might still be there. I felt old and quite empty of feeling or emotion. Conflicting thoughts no longer bombarded my mind ; I was past that. I felt like a person beaten into insensibility. I had been over and over the same ground so often, the same reproaches, the same regrets. That night I slept well but felt no better for it in the morning and Sunday I spent in a kind of stupor. The servants looked oddly at me and no doubt I was acting strangely. But they said nothing.

I thought of telephoning Janet to tell her I was back —just an excuse to speak to her. I was sickened when I realised how nearly I had lost her—thrown away all that she meant to me. But I decided to leave it over for a day or two.

There was something else I had to do, though, and that was ring Fay. I didn't want to but I knew I ought to. The Central Hotel said she had not yet returned. That was something else to worry me! But she must have decided to stay on another day, that was all. Ought I to telephone the hotel we had stayed at? I put off the problem. If she hadn't returned by to-morrow I would ring up then.

When I went to the office the following morning I felt a little better. Not about what had happened, but at the prospect of engrossing myself in work.

My office led on one side to my secretary's office and, immediately in front of it, to a large general office. When I went in to the general office it was empty. Puzzled, I stopped. For a moment I thought I must have my days muddled. Was it Sunday to-day? But no, the usual works' policeman had been at the gate, had saluted me as usual and below me I could hear the overall hum of the factory at work. I went across to my secretary's office, but that too was empty. Shaking my head, I went into my own room.

Jeff Wilson stood up from a chair near the door. He startled me a little.

"Hullo," I said, hanging up my hat. "What's happened this morning? There's no one up here."

"That's right," he said casually. "I sent them away."

"*You* did? Why?"

He went to the door, locked it and put the key in his pocket. I confess I felt a little uneasy.

"What are you doing?"

He stood there with his back to the door, his hands

hanging by his side. I had never realised before how big he was. His eyes seemed hot and angry.

" This is a show-down," he said.

" What are you talking about? " I asked, trying to put some confidence into my voice.

" I think you know all right," he said grimly. " But just in case you're in any doubt, I'll tell you. I saw Fay last Wednesday and she was acting most strangely. I mentioned your name once or twice and she looked even stranger. On Thursday evening I telephoned her hotel. They said she was out. On Friday they told me she hadn't come back. I was worried. I didn't connect you up with it—until I heard that you'd given instructions that you wouldn't be back till Monday. Even then I didn't really think it was any more than a coincidence."

" Wait! " I said. " I don't know what right you have to interfere but, anyway, it's not as bad as you think. Let me—"

He held up his hand. " I'd like to finish. I wanted to speak to you about something else so I rang up Janet to see if you were there."

" Damn you! " I said. " Bringing Janet into it! "

" You might have thought of that before," he remarked coldly. " Janet told me you'd gone off hurriedly on Thursday without saying where you were going. I checked at Fay's hotel and they said someone had called for her in a car. It sounded like you. Well, I was furious, of course. You know I wanted to marry her. But if she wanted to go away for a week-end with a cheap little monkey like you, that was her look-out."

" If that's all you have to say—"

He came a step or two nearer. " It isn't all I have

to say.   On Saturday a call came through to me from a hotel in the country.   Perhaps you know it without my having to say which one !   It was an urgent call. From the proprietor.   It seemed that Fay had handed him a letter addressed to me.   She asked him when the next post was.   He said there was one just going. She told him he'd better hold the letter till the next post, a few hours later.   Then she went off.   Well, the proprietor is a wise old bird.   For some reason he was suspicious.   He didn't know why, but he was.   Fay seemed distracted ; there was a strained ill-look about her.   He thought it strange that you'd left in such a hurry.   He told me it had always been his motto to shoot first and ask questions afterwards.   So do you know what he did? ''

" Well? "   I was not feeling too good.

" He steamed open the letter.   It was a farewell note ; didn't say much except good-bye and would I please see that her parents didn't worry too much. She enclosed a cheque—your cheque.   She thought they might as well have the benefit of it ; you could stand it.''

" What happened? " I asked.   I had to know now.

" The proprietor went after her, brought her back to the hotel on some excuse, put her in his office and— locked her in.   She was yelling and banging at the door, he said, while he was 'phoning.   Could I go up and see her, talk to her?   And that's what happened. I went up and I talked to her.   And after a while I persuaded her to marry me.   It was hard work but I did it.   By then she didn't seem to care what happened.   She's still a bit wild in the head but she'll come through all right.   She's got fine stuff in her. Not like you—all dirt.''

" I'm glad she's all right," I said relieved, ignoring the gibe.

" Sure you're glad ! You've come out very nicely, haven't you. But you don't quite get away with it this time, Dexter Price. Three times now you've been after me, to take away what should have been mine. Three times in a lifetime is too many. There was the garage—remember? "

I stared at him, astonished.

" Oh, yes, I found out about it. It seemed too slick at the time and I nosed around. I thought I'd seen you before. Then I remembered : it was at the Turkish baths. I found the garage man, McCall. He swore he hadn't told anyone else he wanted to sell. Naturally, when you came along and offered more . . . And then the car design. Your whole career's been built on it. Oh, sure, you gave me a job ! Maybe your conscience pricked a little. Well, I'm not complaining about that—not too much. Maybe I was just unlucky in that deal ; and maybe you were a bit too lucky. You're a slick fellow altogether. A good businessman you'd say. I'd call it something else."

He paused. " And now," he went on gently, " there's Fay. And I personally am going to have the greatest pleasure in the world in beating hell out of you. Maybe I can smack out a few devils, like they used to in the olden days. Maybe I can't. But either way, you've got it coming."

He threw off his coat and began to move forward. I retreated to the desk, pressed the bell buttons and grabbed the phone.

Jeff grinned. " I've cut them all. Come out and fight, you rotten little jerk."

His fist caught me on the side of the face. The mark

seemed to burn me.   And then we were at it.

I fought back as well as I could and every now and then landed a blow that seemed to tell.   But I was soft from long inactivity.   For years I had been sitting on my muscles instead of using them.   And Jeff piled in ; there was a driving force in him that smashed through any defence I tried to put up.   We were all over the place, with furniture smashing backwards and forwards.   Soon I must have looked an awful mess. Bruised in every part of my face and body, I was reeling around like a drunken man.

Suddenly I heard a banging on the door.   And then someone shouting : " Are you all right, Mr. Price? "

I hadn't any breath to spare to call back.   I managed to thrust Jeff off but he came back at me again and I fell backwards over a chair.

Someone said : " It's locked.   We'd better break it in."   Something crashed into the door and a few seconds later people were spilling into the room, grabbing Jeff, holding me up.

They put me in my chair, fussing solicitously round me.   Two men were holding Jeff by the arms.   He was glaring ferociously at me as though he wanted to tear me into small pieces.

A man near me said : " We heard the noise downstairs, Mr. Price."

I croaked to Jeff : " I'll give you twenty-four hours to get out of town.   If you're not out I swear you'll be in gaol."

My heart was thumping furiously, like the pendulum of a clock in rapid motion.   I was sore all over and I wanted to retch.

" Don't worry ! " Jeff said.   " I'm going and I'm taking Fay.   But, by God, if you ever bother either of us again I'll gladly die for the pleasure of killing you."

With a powerful movement he threw off the two men and grabbed up his coat. Then, without another glance at me he went through the door and out of my life.

4

I phoned Janet three times and on each occasion I was told she was out. I left a message asking her to ring me but she didn't. Then her letter came, that unbelievable letter.

" . . . I think you ought to know that I've decided not to come back to you . . . "

Of course I went down to see her at once. At first she sent her mother out to say she wouldn't see me, but I sent the old lady back with a message that I was going to see her if I had to break down the house to do it. And so at last she sat there in the drawing-room facing me.

Her cool eyes regarded me levelly. " Well, Dexter? " she said.

" Surely it's for me to say ' well ', isn't it? You suddenly act in this peculiar way, refuse to speak to me or see me, send me an extraordinary letter . . ."

" Was it so extraordinary? I should have thought it was quite natural for me to refuse to return to you after what happened."

" What *did* happen that upset you so much?" I asked.

" I see. You want to find out how much I know, before you commit yourself any further. Is that it? You needn't worry. I think I know pretty well the whole story. I should think everyone in the city knows it by now, about you and Jeff Wilson. And I have a few contacts there, you know. Perhaps they don't all know about the girl, about the reason for that happening between you and Jeff. But I know."

"Old man Marsh told you, I suppose," I said contemptuously.

"Does it matter so much who told me?"

She looked at me curiously. "You were packing to go for her that night when I—when I came home, weren't you? You were angry with me because I was delaying you." The scorn in her voice was terrible. "Oh, Dex, how could you?"

For an instant then I thought she was going to break down. That would have given me my chance—to comfort her, to tell her that it was all past. But she recovered herself and sat there calm again and impenetrable in the armour she had assumed.

I stood up. "Is there nothing I can say, then? What about the children? Have you thought of them?"

"They won't be any worse off. You never had much time for them, anyway. You should have married a machine and—and had small machines for children. Then you could have lived with them all at your factory and been really happy."

"You are bitter, Janet," I said gently.

She threw up her head. "And why not? Haven't I a right to be?"

"Janet, it's all over now"

"Not for me it isn't. For you, yes. You had what you wanted and now it's over. For me it's only just beginning."

Her tone was quite determined.

I said : " I'd like to see the children."

For a moment I thought she was going to refuse. Then : " All right," she agreed, and left the room. A few minutes later I could hear them all coming. They burst in excitedly.

" It's Daddy," Elizabeth cried, and ran over to me. Children and dogs are much the same. If they belong to you they keep the same lovely enthusiasm for you whatever you've done. It was nice to feel her arms round my neck.

Then Fenton, the eldest. He was not quite too old to be kissed. " Hullo, son."

" Hullo, Dad."

And three-year-old Walter.

" Well, children, are you having a nice time with Mummy and Granny? "

A chorus of yesses was followed by three confused streams of chatter as they all began to tell me what they had been doing.

" Are you going to stay with us now, Daddy? " Elizabeth asked.

I looked over their heads at Janet, but her eyes were quite cold and unyielding.

" No, dear. Not just now. I have to go back to town and work. But you be very good children and I'll send you all some presents."

" We'd rather you were here," Fenton said.

" I'm learning to play Granny's piano," Elizabeth said. " I can use two fingers. If you stayed I'd play for you, like Mummy."

" That's wonderful ! " I said. " I'll—come down and hear you sometime. So you practise hard."

" Come on now, children," Janet said. " Daddy has to go. Say good-bye."

She shepherded them out of the room and turned back to me.

Wearily I went to the door.

Turning, I asked: "Are you going to get a divorce?"

She shook her head. "I don't know yet. I'm not going to think about it."

"Good-bye," I said. "I know it's too late to say anything now. But there isn't anyone but you. There never really was, and there never will be. Come back if you can, Janet. I'll be waiting—and hoping."

I wallowed in self-pity for the next five months. Twice I went down to visit the children, but Janet wouldn't see me while I was there.

Mother Playfair seemed quite sorry for me. "You're a foolish man, Dexter," she said. "And I can't blame Janet for feeling as she does." She shook her small, wise old head. "All the same, I'd like you to make up. It's nice for me to have them here, never did like the house with all the rooms empty and only me to live in them. But it's not right to break up the family. There's too much of it going on. I don't like it. Maybe she'll come round," she added gloomily.

I looked at her thinking that it must be pretty upsetting for a mother to see her daughter's life breaking up. Somehow she wasn't looking so well as she used to—the irrepressible twinkle was no longer in her eyes. I supposed she was really getting old at last.

"You don't look too well," I told her. "Perhaps the children are too much for you ; you're doing more than you should."

"I do feel a bit off-colour," she admitted. She

sighed. " I don't know : things seem to worry me so much more than they used to. Just the years creeping up, I suppose."

" Nonsense ! " I exclaimed. " We'll have you for another fifty years yet."

" Well, for heaven's sake get your wife back then," she snapped unreasonably. " If you don't, there'll be a divorce—and I shouldn't like that."

" What *can* I do? " I asked despairingly. " If there was anything I could do, I would. After all, what I did wasn't so very terrible. Men just are like that, that's all. You must agree it could have been worse."

" Is that the kind of recommendation you'd employ a man on? " she said tartly. " You'll have to offer something better than that."

I returned home no better off than before.

At the factory the gossip and the rumours seemed to have died down. People no longer gave me curious glances whenever I appeared. It had been a hard time living that down and it had taken some courage to carry on as though nothing had happened.

Thinking about Janet I wondered how it would be if she did divorce me. The idea was unbearable but I supposed she might just as well as carry on like this. I imagined her married to someone else. No, damn it all, the idea was monstrous. And yet I had contemplated doing the same thing myself! I began to realise how deeply hurt she must have been.

Three or four weeks after my last visit I had a telegram :

Mother seriously ill, asking for you. Please come at once. Janet.

I did not even consider what this new development

portended but drove down immediately. When I had told the old lady she didn't look well, I hadn't thought for an instant that there could be anything seriously wrong.

Janet met me at the door. She had been crying. I immediately sensed that her attitude towards me had softened amongst whatever other emotions she was experiencing.

" Is it bad? " I asked.

" She's been unconscious since I sent you the telegram. She was asking for you just before. Oh, Dex, she's going to die. The doctor says there's no chance. She knew it herself, I think."

" Steady ! " I put my arm round her shoulders as we went in and though she stiffened slightly, she made no effort to draw away.

" Is the doctor here? "

" No, I'm to call him up if she recovers consciousness or if—anything happens. He doesn't know how long it will be and there wouldn't be much point in his staying around, waiting."

The children were being put to bed and I went up to see them. For them, they were impressively hushed and sober. Perhaps they could sense the approach of death.

" Is Granny very sick, Daddy? " Elizabeth asked solemnly.

" She's deaded," Walter declared realistically.

Elizabeth, near to tears, upbraided him. " She is not so, you wicked little boy."

" Hush, darling," Janet said. " It isn't wicked to talk about being dead. Everyone has to die some-time."

" But Granny isn't dead ? " Fenton said, puzzled.

" No, dear," Janet blew her nose. " She's sleeping now."

When they were all in bed we sat in the lounge together. Neither of us spoke for a long time.

At last Janet said : " Dexter—"

I looked up, not even sure that she had spoken, we had been so enwrapped in the silence.

" Dexter, you know that Mother wanted us to be together again, wanted me to go back to you? "

" Yes, she told me that."

" Do you still want me back? "

A warm glow sprang inside me. I smiled for the first time for weeks. " Want you? Of course I do ! I've thought of nothing else ever since you left."

A tiny smile crept along the corners of her mouth. " Not even your business? "

" Oh, well ! " . . . I laughed. " Will you, Janet? We could begin again, forget everything. . . . If only you could ! " I went over to her and put my hands on her shoulders. " Will you ? "

She looked searchingly up at me. " I promised Mother I would."

" Is that the only reason? Surely there must be something between us yet, Janet. Some small spark? You can't wipe out everything in one stupid moment. I won't let you down again, I promise. And I still feel the same way about you . . ."

" All right," she said, putting her hands on mine. " It has been rather lonely, Dex."

I bent and kissed her.

A thin cry interrupted us. At first we thought it was one of the children but it came again, a feeble call : " Jan-et ! " It was Mrs. Playfair.

We hurried in together.

The old lady lay shrunken and small, swallowed up in the bed.

"There you are, Janet. I've been asleep."

"Yes, dear." Janet took her hand and patted it. I stood by her side.

"And you're here, Dexter. Good. I wanted to see you again."

"You'll be up in the morning," I said. "Bouncing around as strong as ever."

She shot a glance up at me from under her wrinkled eyelids. "I'm not a child." Her voice was weak. "I know I'm going." A feeble smile crossed her face. "And where I'm going, money wouldn't be any use— not even to you, Dexter. Now, tell me—are you two going to stop this silly nonsense? You'll have the house, Janet. Was your grandfather's. But don't live in it. Not just you and the children. Sell it. Go back with your man. Promise me, now! He's a fool, but some are worse. No recommendation, Dexter. . . . For better or worse . . . Yours now . . ." Her voice slowed down, faltered. Talking had been too great an effort.

"I have promised, darling." Janet bent over the small form. "I'm going back with the children. Don't talk any more now. Just rest."

"That's right." Her eyes were closing. "Nice . . . house, full children . . . but go back . . ." Her eyes closed.

They did not open again.

FIVE

I

OFTEN, on the occasions when I came home to lunch I could hear Elizabeth practising at the piano.

Ever since her days at her grandmother's house she had been tinkering about with the instrument. At that age we neither encouraged nor discouraged her : she was far too young for us to consider her seriously at all and as long as she didn't make a nuisance of herself we didn't mind how much she played about with it.

It was interesting, though, to note her reactions compared with those of the other children. Fenton merely ignored the piano. He hadn't even the urge to touch the keys at all. Walter, on the other hand, even as he grew up, would sometimes throw himself down on the stool and sweep his fingers along the keys. Then he would crash out a few jarring chords—or, rather, conglomerations of unrelated notes—at the same time chanting some barbaric, tuneless song at the top of his voice.

But Elizabeth was quite different. From the earliest time she approached the instrument with something akin to devotion. She would stand shyly by its side and touch it lovingly as though she might coax its music out of it. Or she would watch her mother playing, staring fascinated at the keyboard. At about seven she was quite obviously looking for better things than two-finger gallops and we found a music-teacher for her. For two or three years her playing was completely normal—just a small girl practising monotonously at the piano with her brothers complaining automatically now and then at the everlasting scales. She was however persistent and determined. Though all of us longed at times for her to do so, she never skimped her practising ; we tried to suffer it with a good grace.

The change in her playing was so gradual, so imperceptible that we noticed it only after it had actually happened, almost as though it had occurred overnight.

We were sitting in the next room while Elizabeth was practising. Suddenly the scale stopped.

" Phew !   Glad that's finished ! " Fenton said.

Then a few more notes were struck.   " Spoke too soon," Fenton groaned.

I put down my paper.   " Listen ! " I said.

It was a small simple air but it was pretty.   More than that it was being played with some accomplishment.   All of us could tell that, though Janet was the only one with any musical knowledge.

Fenton looked puzzled.   " Who's playing now? " he said.

" It's your sister still, of course," Janet said.   " Why that's *good* ! "

" It is kind of pretty," Fenton conceded.   " But that can't be Liz."

" She can't play for nuts," Walter put in sweepingly, looking up from the floor where he was wrestling with the dog.

Almost with one accord we stood up and went over to the door, peering into the next room.

Elizabeth was playing without music, her eyes unseeing, her face flushed and happy with the music she was producing. She did not see us and we all stood quietly. As she finished we gave her a round of applause. Startled, she turned to us, unable to decide whether we were making fun of her or not.

6

" That was fine," I said.

" It was lovely, dear," Janet added. " You're coming on splendidly."

For a small girl it had, in fact, been a striking performance.

From that time on we knew we had an artiste with us. Not a genius, perhaps, but one who would, with the proper teaching, become an accomplished concert-hall player. I was very proud of her. With my help she would go right to the top.

Sometimes I would take Fenton down to the factory and walk him through the long machine lines. " One day," I used to say, " this will be all yours. The others will have an interest too, of course, but you're the eldest : you'll be in charge."

" Yes, father," he would say, but I never detected any enthusiasm in his voice. Oh, well, I told myself, it was too early yet to expect him to take any interest in these things. All the same, I was a little disappointed, hoping without avail that he might at least show a leaning towards mechanical things. But his only enjoyment seemed to lie in animals and crops ; if we ever got near a farm he was immediately in his element.

What about Walter, I wondered? Where would his interests lie? But Walter gave no indication of having any serious interests at all. He was the kind of boy who was always in some kind of trouble or other. It wasn't that he was unintelligent. In his way he was quite bright and alert. But he only seemed to be interested in the more exciting things of life. In school he was simply too lazy to care. Somehow the notion of being a rich man's child had passed over the other two and landed squarely on him. From the earliest age he seemed to have the impression that he would never need to work.

And he was Janet's favourite. Perhaps that was natural since they had nearly died together at his unexpected birth. Not that she showed her favour in front of the others. But I knew. Nor did she encourage him in his lazy or troublesome ways. It was just the opposite—and she was the only one with any influence at all over him. But she couldn't help taking his part when anyone else attacked him.

He never seemed to have any vice in him, but plenty of devilment. At school he was always fighting —and usually victoriously. And he was the leader of a small gang of toughs—all of them a very different type from himself. But school was dull and gangs and trouble were fun! Windows smashed—shop goods wrecked—people knocked into and tripped up . . . I was constantly paying compensation, apologising. And Walter was constantly being chastised—without the slightest effect ; all punishment he treated cheerfully but contemptuously. If I talked to him severely he merely sat there watching me, his eyes mocking, his manner subtly infused with boredom or indifference. My patience with him wore steadily thinner.

Gradually my business interests were increasing. Since my lesson over the Airdex fiasco I moved more slowly but with more confidence. I built up my power step by step, steadily widening my scope, acquiring my small financial empire. I collected directorships as some men collect pictures or antiques. My first and foremost love remained the factory, but other things now used up much of my time. As we went along we became more and more independent, acquiring factories to manufacture our own spare parts, acquiring even a bakery to make the food for our canteen. These concerns, in addition to providing our own requirements, created a subsidiary trade of their own. And so it went on, one thing leading to another, even to shops for the workers and then the manufacture of goods for the shops, and so more shops to absorb the goods . . .

It would be useless for me to deny that I was becoming a person of considerable power and importance. Once catch on to the swing of the pendulum going in the right direction and there is no stopping it until it reaches the end of its momentum. There seemed hardly a thing I could do wrong in business. And, too, the more successful one is the more chance one has of taking whatever opportunities are offered. It is easy to say that opportunity knocks only once—not so easy for a poor man to be able to risk taking the opportunity for what it is. And of course I was smart ; I was always that. Smartness is a normal ingredient of success and certainly I was both smart and successful.

Even Janet had to admit that I was achieving what I had set out to achieve. But while I gloried in it, Janet, I think, was secretly amused by it. Perhaps, I thought at times, she took it all a little too much for granted. But I had had to work for my success . . . Anyway, we undoubtedly had our full complement of servants now to make things as easy as possible for her ; I could hardly take her seriously when sometimes she said it was as much hard work looking after the servants as it would be looking after the house without them . . .

I was watching Elizabeth playing during one of her

lessons. Her teacher was a young girl possessed of quite an outstanding talent but little money. She was an attractive little thing. Elizabeth would do very well with her until she was a little older and outgrew her. One did not want to rush things ; the best teachers could wait until the ground work had been filled in.

It was pleasant to see them together, the child and the girl, both earnestly engrossed in the piano, Elizabeth's hair brown like her mother's, and the girl's fair hair bobbing about together. At first the girl, Virginia Field, had been embarrassed by my presence. But she was used to me now. I liked to sit and watch them—not that I could indulge myself in sparing the time often.

She *was* a pretty little thing ! I found myself nodding my head in time to the music. Such a graceful figure ! It was nice that one could stare at someone's back without being thought rude.

I gave a start and looked up. Janet was standing at the door.

I went across on tip-toe. " Hullo," I whispered. " I didn't see you there."

" I know," she replied. " What's happened to you? Having a day off? "

" No—I just thought I'd take in a bit of Elizabeth's lesson. Very interesting, you know. She's doing well, isn't she? "

" Yes." Janet was looking across at them.

" Oh well," I said. " I'll be off now."

" Good-bye, dear." She offered me her cheek. " I'll stay : I want to have a word with Virginia."

Over dinner that evening I said : " Elizabeth is doing very well, isn't she? Nice girl that. Virginia, I mean."

"Yes," Janet agreed. Then she added casually:
"Oh, by the way, I've told her we won't be needing
her any more. I gave her a cheque as a parting
present. I thought you wouldn't mind; she does
need it."

"Who's this?" I asked, not following.

"Virginia Field, dear. I thought we were talking
about her."

I put down my knife and fork. "You told her we
wouldn't be needing her any more? But why? I'm
afraid I don't understand."

"Well, I thought it was time Elizabeth had someone
a little more—mature. I thought we might see if
Waldo Fleck will take her."

"But this is absurd," I said. "To just send her
away like that—"

"She understood, dear. And I've given her one
or two introductions to other people."

"But still!—I do think you might have consulted
me."

"I am sorry. I thought you'd agree."

I digested the matter in silence for a while and then
put my knife and fork down again. A suspicion had
crossed my mind.

"Why," I said, "I do believe you sent her away
on my account. Did you think I was going to fall for
her?"

"Of course not, dear. Don't be silly!" But she
looked a little uneasily at me.

I began to laugh. "I ought to be annoyed," I
declared. "But I'm amused."

Janet rang the bell and the dishes were cleared.
Neither of us referred to the matter again. Well, perhaps I had had a twinge, I admitted to myself. Only

the slightest twinge, of course. I sighed. Janet was a wise woman . . .

2

Years flew past like leaves in Autumn. When the pictures slowed to a recognisable pace, Fenton was talking to me, a much older Fenton.

"Father, I wish you hadn't done it. Made arrangements I mean, about my going into the factory."

"But Fenton," I said, "that's the only way to tackle these things. One has to start at the bottom and work up, see everything there is to be seen, so that when one gets to the top one knows what it's all about. I learnt by growing up with it. But as soon as I went into something I knew nothing about, I flopped."

Fenton looked at the floor. Regarding him, I felt a surge of pleasure that this young man could be my son. He was a fine young fellow, straight, well-made, good-looking enough without being uncomfortably so—I wouldn't have had him any different. He was everything that I was afraid Walter would never be.

"That's not what I mean, Father," he said quietly. "It was just that—well, I didn't want to go into the factory at all."

I stared unbelievably at him. Then I sat down slowly. "I'm sorry, son," I said. "I'm not following you very well."

"Well," he said, looking as if he was about to take a plunge into deep water. "I was thinking I'd like to go in for farming."

"I see. And the business—all that I've built up for you and the others—that's just to go hang?"

" I don't say that.   There are the others—"

" Who? Do you think Elizabeth is going to run a factory? She's a pianist, and a good one : and that's her career. And Walter? Well, it's hard to tell yet, but somehow I can't see Walter taking over the business. He might, perhaps, if you were there to help him, to steady him.   But by himself !—No, I don't think so."

" Well, even so, Dad, a fellow has to live his own life. You picked cars when you started but my interest's in farming, not cars.   Surely there's nothing wrong with that ! "

My dreams were tottering, ready to crash around me.

" Listen, boy," I said.   " Sit down.   That's right. You know success in this world isn't an easy thing. Everyone can't get it.   Some people don't suit it anyway.   And I guess others just don't set about it in the right way.   But you—you haven't any of this to worry about.   Your success is ready-made for you. I made it ; I've slogged hard for it.   All you have to do is to learn a few things and then, when the time's ready, step into my shoes.   You'll have unlimited possibilities then.   And if you still want to go farming, why there'll be absolutely nothing to stop you ; you'll be able to buy a dozen farms if you want to."

Fenton looked stubborn.   " That's not what I mean by farming ; I don't want to farm on factory methods."

" You'll be able to farm any way you want—if you've first got your business running properly.   But— farming just by itself !   Where would that get you? There's no real prosperity in farming, except perhaps on a large scale."

" I'm not bothered about prosperity, about what you call success, Dad."

I snorted.   " That's easy to say."   I wondered if he

got his ideas from Janet. " But you've never known anything except prosperity. Anyway, let's not argue about that. The business means a lot to me, you know. I've always hoped it would go on, become one of those family traditions."

Fenton looked uncomfortable. " I don't—"

" Just one more word on farming," I broke in. " You can't start without capital, you know."

He flushed. " You mean you wouldn't stake me? I see—"

I put up my hand. " Not so fast, son. I don't mean that at all. But why not let's leave it like this. You come into the business, learn all you can and see how you get on. And when you want your farm I'll see you through. It'll make me very happy, Fenton, to have you there. How about it? "

He stood up and went over to the window. Opening it, he leaned out. At last he closed it again and turned round to face me. " All right, Father," he said in his quiet way.

3

Elizabeth gave her first recital when she was eighteen. It must have been a frightening, yet a rather wonderful experience for her. We were there in strength—and I saw to it that the critics were there too. But I needn't have worried : they had no need to force their praise. Elizabeth was undoubtedly a ' find '. She had completely fulfilled her early promise and, in one bound, was set straight on to the ladder of success . . .

It was on her nineteenth birthday that she told us she wanted to marry John Warren.

We had met him then, at her party, for the first time. I hadn't paid particular attention to him because there were so many different people moving around. Elizabeth just introduced him with a: " Daddy, this is John Warren," and I shook hands with him and promptly forgot him. Until the bombshell!

I was with Janet at the time. We were in my study taking a few minutes rest from the youthful hurly-burly of the party.

The door opened and Elizabeth looked in. She seemed radiant, her eyes bright, her soft brown hair dancing at her neck ; just like her mother all over again. " Oh, there you both are. Sober-sides! " she exclaimed, slipping into the room.

" We're just collecting ourselves for a little more exuberance, dear," Janet said.

" Pooh! " said Elizabeth. " I know—you're not as young as you used to be ! Anyway, it's a lovely party. And I'm glad I've found you both together because I have something to announce."

She hesitated, blushing a little.

" Go on, darling," Janet encouraged her.

" Well—oh, I do hope you'll like it. John Warren has asked me to marry him—and I've said yes."

Our reception of the news can hardly have been what she had hoped for. We were both struck motionless ; I was actually about to swallow and I even stopped doing that.

At last I managed to strangle out a few words: " He . . . he . . . you did what? "

" Well, of course he's going to ask you first, Daddy, but—"

" Elizabeth," I said, " who is this boy? "

" John? But I introduced you to him to-night."

" You didn't tell me he'd asked you to—to marry him."

" He hadn't, then."

" Darling," Janet said softly, " why haven't we met him before? "

" I don't know. No special reason. I've been wanting to bring him along to meet you for some time. Only the chance never seemed to occur. And I—I didn't think he was going to ask me so soon. We've been out together quite a bit. He's an awfully nice person. He was at college with Fenton—until his father died. He had to leave and go to work then : there wasn't enough money to carry on."

" And what exactly does Mr. John Warren do then?" I asked. " For a living, I mean? Besides asking attractive heiresses to marry him? "

Elizabeth flared up. " If you're going to be rude about him I won't discuss it any more. John has a job with the Manuflex Wire Company."

" Oh, yes." I knew of them, though we didn't deal with them ourselves. Quite a good, small, progressive firm. " And what sort of a job is it? Managing Director—or office boy? "

" You're being beastly," Elizabeth said. " I was afraid it would be like this." She bit her lip. " He's a clerk but he's expecting a promotion soon. And anyway what does that matter? Everyone doesn't start out by being a millionaire."

I stood up. " The whole thing's absurd. I don't know why we're even discussing it. In the first place you're too young to marry."

" Bosh ! " said my daughter. " Lots of people get married at nineteen. And we could wait a bit."

" In the second place," I went on, ignoring her, " he

doesn't sound at all the kind of man we would expect you to marry. If he's a clerk on small pay it's going to take him a long time to amount to anything. Perhaps you don't understand these things, Elizabeth, but we're at the top now. Or thereabouts. It took us quite a while to get there. And when you're at the top you stay there. You don't wander down because the view looks pleasant from where you're standing and then try to climb up again."

" Well, if that isn't sheer, undiluted snobbery, I don't know what is. As if money was so important ! "

" It is. And in the third place, there's your career to think of. You're doing pretty well, Elizabeth. Surely you don't want to get married just now and spoil all that? There'll be plenty of time for marrying later."

" Listen, Daddy," she said earnestly. " I'm not a career girl. Oh, yes, I know I've got a career if I want one. I'm not too modest to think that. But however brilliant the future, whatever wonderful things it has for me in the way of concerts, if the choice is between that and marriage, then the piano doesn't stand a chance. And there won't be plenty of time for marriage later : marriage is where you find it. And there's one small point you've completely overlooked—I happen to be in love with John."

The silence ricochetted round the room.

" We'll talk about it later, dear," Janet broke in.

" Won't you even see him? " Elizabeth said despairingly.

" I can't see the point," I said. " It wouldn't make any—"

The door had slammed and Elizabeth had vanished on what had sounded like a sob.

I knew exactly what I was going to do and so I didn't discuss the matter much with Janet. Probably she would side with Elizabeth to some extent, for romanticism is the life blood of a woman, and I did not want to hear the foolish, illogical, womanly arguments that would surely emerge. I knew what was best for Elizabeth.

Fancy, I thought, if those talents of hers, of which I was so proud, should be wasted by some fantastic early marriage! The notion appalled me. Anyone could achieve marriage and there was nothing brilliant about the birth of children. But to be a famous pianist —there was real achievement.

It was true that Elizabeth thought at the moment that marriage was more important to her. But she would get over it. One day she would thank me for what I had done for her. And as for John Warren— there would be other men, plenty of men far more eligible than he was. Later she would be able to take her choice, if she still wished it. John was definitely not the type I had had in mind for my daughter; however, since she said she was in love with him he seemed to constitute the immediate problem.

The next day I looked up what available information there was about the Manuflex Wire Company. The guiding light and Managing Director was a man named Frederick T. Hobbs. I made up my mind to call on Mr. Hobbs.

My secretary made an appointment for me without specifying any reason for the interview. I knew that Mr. Hobbs would be glad to see me; a contact like that would be worth having by a progressive firm of that size.

He met me at the door of his office with outstretched

hand, beaming widely. "This is an unexpected pleasure, Mr. Price. Come and sit down. Cigar?"

I accepted one and lit it. Mr. Hobbs was an older man than I had imagined but the eyes were keen, the face shrewd.

"I wondered," I said, "if we might do a little business together some time."

His eyes shone. "Delighted!" he exclaimed.

I asked him a few questions about his firm's products and he fussed briskly round, calling his secretary to produce papers and pamphlets.

At last I thought it was time to get down to the real purpose of my visit—before giving him any definite orders. His mouth should be on the line now, ready to snap eagerly at it!

When we were alone again I said, examining the tip of my cigar: "Oh, there's one small thing I wanted to talk to you about. Nothing to do with business, really. Just a small favour . . ."

Slightly puzzled, he said: "I'll be glad to do anything I can."

"This is confidential," I told him and he nodded. "You have a young man named Warren working for you. John Warren. He's a clerk?"

"Have we?" he asked. "I don't know off-hand, of course, but I can look it up. What about the young man, Mr. Price?"

"Just this," I said carefully. "I understand you have a South American connection."

"That is so."

"You'd be doing me a great service if you would send Warren to South America to work for you."

He looked blankly at me. Then he smiled. "I take it you're serious? Yes, you are. Well, it's rather an extraordinary request. Perhaps you could give me some more information about the reason for it."

"All right," I said. "I will. I haven't anything against the young man myself. Don't think that. Not in himself. In fact, I scarcely know him. But the truth is that he's been paying rather unwelcome attentions to my daughter. As a matter of fact she says she's in love with him."

"You say unwelcome attentions. Do you mean he forces himself on her?"

"He wants to marry her," I said. "Of course, the whole thing's absurd. I thought that if he went away for a year or two, she'd soon get over it. You know how it is at that age. They say that absence makes the heart more fond, but of course it does nothing of the sort. Not at that age and stage. One soon goes on to new interests."

Mr. Hobbs shook his head again. "You must forgive me if I'm unduly obtuse, Mr. Price. You say they're in love and want to get married. What's the objection?"

"Well, surely, Mr. Hobbs!—They're hardly suited. . . . After all, my daughter! . . . But even apart from that—my daughter has rather an unusual talent as a pianist. She's given a few recitals already ; they prophesy great things for her. I couldn't let her ruin that by marrying this—this clerk. Surely you must see that?"

Mr. Hobbs placed his hands flat on his desk. He said deliberately and clearly : "Mr. Price, I'm very sorry but I can't help you."

I frowned. "I don't understand. All I'm asking—"

"I know exactly what you're asking and I can't do it."

I compressed my lips. " May I ask why not? "

" Simply because, Mr. Price, I don't believe in interfering in other people's lives."

" But it's my daughter—"

" I hardly think that justifies it."

I stood up. " Very well. I scarcely thought you'd refuse. Those orders . . . I shall have to think them over a bit more. If you're so unco-operative, I'm afraid we won't be very happy doing business together."

" Good ! " he said standing up. " That's what I expected. And if you really think I'd do business with you as a bribe !—" He drew a deep breath. " Why, you little tin-pot dictator, trying to order people's lives around ! I begin to suspect that this young Warren is far too good for any daughter of yours."

I was furious, but pretended to be quite calm. I took my hat and went to the door. " You'll regret this," I told him, and went out

I spent most of the afternoon with my lawyer.

" Listen," I told him. " I want to buy a company." I gave him the name of Hobbs' concern.

" I want to buy it privately," I said. " Will I stretch to that? I don't want it connected with Pridex just now. Later on, it won't matter and perhaps Pridex can take it over. But at the moment I don't want my name mentioned at all. If the Company buys it, it'll have to be disclosed to the shareholders. That's why I want to get it privately. Understand ? Buy it in your name for me. That'll do. I'll give you a Power of Attorney."

He gave me a curious glance.

" It's all right," I said. " There's nothing crooked

about it. I want one of their employees and I can't get him any other way."

" You must want him awfully badly. Can a man be worth all that? "

" I don't want him," I said. " I want to get rid of him."

" Well, well," he said facetiously. " Now we have reached a new level of business ! When a man buys a company to give someone the push—"

" It's Elizabeth," I told him. " This fellow wants to marry her and I don't want him to. That's all."

" She's under age, anyway," he remarked. " Needs your consent."

" But I don't want to see her unhappy. Send him away and she'll forget all about him."

He whistled softly. " You'd do a lot for that girl, wouldn't you."

" Of course," I said. " Anything."

He called me up on the telephone.
" Hobbs won't sell."
" At what price? "
" At any price. He's just not interested in selling."
" I see." I digested this for a moment and then said : " Can you find out for me the major firms he deals with ? "
" Yes, I think so."
" Do that, will you, and let me have them as soon as you can? "

There were more ways than one of killing the cat. Meaning Mr. Hobbs.

The list he sent me showed that there were four main buyers from the Manuflex Wire Company. Three of them dealt with us; I had hoped for that. They bought from Hobbs but we in turn were the largest buyers of their products. I smiled to myself; only one factor was involved now—the prevailing keenness of competition.

I went to each of the three manufacturers in turn. I was sorry, I said—in strict confidence—that the quality of their goods had been decreasing slightly of late. They protested. All their work was the same as it had ever been and subjected to the same vigorous tests as before. Well, perhaps, I said, but naturally I must take it as we found it for our use. They dealt with the Manuflex Wire Company, I understood, and I had heard some poor reports of their products; no doubt the cause lay there. Oh no, they said, they had always found the Manuflex products very sound. Well, there it was, I shrugged; we should like an undertaking from them to discontinue further orders from that Company. Otherwise— And after some argument I had my way; there was no option, really.

The "squeeze", as I called it, took some time to get properly going. But during that period I persuaded Elizabeth to see less of her young man, on the pretext that if she did this for a while and they still both felt the same way I would no longer stand in her way.

Then one day Mr. Frederick Hobbs tried to make an appointment to see me. He said it was urgent. I smiled grimly to myself and refused to see him or even speak to him. He was beginning to feel the effectiveness of my weight. A few days later he burst peremptorily into my office and accosted me.

" Please ! " he begged. " Just give me a few minutes. There's something I want to ask you. We're losing orders fast. The firms that are stopping their orders all deal with you. I've found that out. Have you got anything to do with it? "

" That's an extraordinary accusation," I said. " I think you'd better be careful."

" The whole thing is highly suspicious."

" I don't know what you're talking about," I said, " but if you want to repeat that to anyone I'll be glad to sue you from here to next year."

" You're a hard man, Price. Some time ago I had an offer made to buy me out. If that was on your behalf, would you care to make me another offer now."

" Don't be a fool, Hobbs. I haven't any desire to buy your miniature concern."

" By God," he flared, " I've got a good mind to tell that young man you're so worried about exactly what you came to ask me."

" Do that," I said evenly. " But when you've done it I promise you that I shall ruin you completely, extinguish you—if it takes me the rest of my life and costs me everything I possess. I could do it, you know."

He went without another word.

A few days later I thought the time was ripe to make a fresh offer, a considerably reduced one. Nor was I surprised when my lawyer told me it had been accepted.

I put my own manager into the firm in place of the departed Mr. Hobbs, gave it new life and through the manager requested Elizabeth's young friend, John Warren, to sign a five-year contract. To avoid suspicion on his part I also put several other members of the staff under contract. John was elated, Elizabeth said. It meant the firm had confidence in him. He had a rise in pay and a sliding scale in his contract . . .

There was just one small point in the contract he

had overlooked: the firm had the right to send him abroad if it wished. And soon afterwards it did so wish. A transfer to South America. Oh, not for long: it probably wouldn't be for more than six months, it was explained to him. . . . Once there, the period could easily be extended—and extended again.

I did not think we should be worried again by Mr. John Warren for some time to come.

Elizabeth grieved a little at first. But the separation would not be for long, she thought. I decided that it might be a good idea if she went away for a while. The most natural way to get her to acquiesce in this was for her to be offered a recital tour. Since one was not forthcoming just then I arranged for a suitable offer to be made; the condition was that I would make up any loss of receipts. The only thing was that Elizabeth could not go off alone; in any case she needed a companion. My sister's husband had died some time before, leaving her with no ties and not a great deal of money. I asked her to accompany Elizabeth and she agreed readily. Elizabeth succumbed to the offer—and away they went.

Meanwhile two or three letters came from John Warren. I returned them unopened with a letter of my own. I said that Elizabeth had decided to devote herself to her own career and had asked me to say that she thought it would be best if they did not correspond any more. I had previously instructed my sister, Clare, to do everything in her power to get hold of any letters Elizabeth wrote and offer to post them herself. Not receiving letters would first worry them both and then aggravate them.

Then John Warren wrote back very stiffly to me

enclosing a message for Elizabeth. It said, bitterly :

> . . . It seems the whole thing between us was a mistake. Never mind, the South American girls are very interesting in their way—quite a warm way . . .

It couldn't have suited my purpose better ; I sent it on. It might bewilder Elizabeth but it would probably be quite effective. Pride is such an easily affronted instinct . . .

I hadn't any compunction about what I was doing. Elizabeth would be unhappy for a short time. But soon she would lose herself in her work, find her happiness in her success. That would be my justification.

There was no need for me to make up any losses on that tour. There were no losses. The whole thing was a triumph, for Elizabeth. From then on there was no looking back for her. She went from one success to another. From recitals to concert playing. The plaudits of one famous conductor followed in the wake of another's. I used to read out the notices to Janet. Following her success was one of the most enjoyable things in my life. What greater proof could there be, I thought, that I had acted for the best? During the war, with all the troop concerts she gave, she reached fresh pinnacles . . .

I missed her, though. We had not seen her for a long time . . .

A picture came to me, a picture that I had not seen before, a picture in which I had no part. I saw Elizabeth ; she was finishing a concert. She wore a white evening dress, her brown hair hanging to her shoulders. I saw past the lovely concert piano, the conductor, his hand raised . . . silence . . . a hushed stillness from the large audience . . . then the hand

sweeping down and the piano coming in for the climax
. . . the orchestra sweeping in . . . the sudden surge
and sense of power, of grandeur. It was over. The
last note . . . the moment hung in stupendous silence
. . . the wild burst of applause. Elizabeth stood up,
smiled, bowed . . . to the conductor . . . to the
audience again . . .

She was sitting in her hotel room. Her manager
was there, a thin little man with a worried face. Not
that he had anything to worry about. " You were
wonderful," he said. " As always."

Elizabeth said: " I wasn't and you know I
wasn't."

" Oh, but really ! " he protested.

" It's no use, Alex. I know how it is when I'm
playing. Oh, yes, my execution's good. Technically,
I suppose, I'm as perfect as I shall ever be. But I've
nothing to put in it, nothing to give. No heart."

The little man looked uncomfortable. He shifted
restlessly round the room, the beautifully furnished
room, picking up an ornament here and there and
letting it slide gently down again. " The audience
liked you. They called you back four times. More,
only you wouldn't come."

Her smile was bitter. " They're not very discerning,
my public. They like to see me play. It must seem
romantic to them, the girl in white playing up there on
the platform with the great orchestra hanging on her
notes . . . What do they know of how I feel, of how
empty I am inside? "

She leaned back wearily ; she did look tired, poor
girl.

The little man was suddenly solicitous. " Elizabeth,
what is it? What is troubling you? I didn't know it

was so bad. Come, what is it? You can tell your Alexis."

" That's just it," she sighed. " I can't. I can't even tell myself. I don't know. Oh, I'm just a fool, I guess, a foolish girl who's not grateful for what she has. After all, I'm a success, aren't I? "

" Of course, you are, my dear. A tremendous success."

" That ought to mean something, oughtn't it? You should hear my father talking about success. He's an expert. Poor Daddy! Oh, I'm lonely, Alex—lonely. Have you ever been lonely? "

He was about to speak but she motioned to him. " No, it doesn't mean being alone. One can be lonely and surrounded by crowds, stifled by crowds. That's what's wrong with me. Success! Crowds! Oh, God!"

There were tears in her eyes. She brushed them angrily away.

" Elizabeth! " Alex said, inadequately.

" Did you know," she said, " that I was nearly married once ? His name was John. I was nineteen."

" What happened? " He perked up his head.

" Oh, I don't know. I never did know. We got separated. He had to follow his job. What happened then? I don't know. Things intervened. It doesn't matter now. I was going to marry him, Alex, marry him and have a family."

Remembering, her eyes, wet still with the unshed tears, lit up.

Softly she said : " A home and a family. That's all I ever wanted. Just a small home . . ."

She put her hands before her, fingers outstretched. Harshly she said : " Why was I given these? Why did

I ever play the piano? My public! . . . Crowds!
. . . And loneliness! . . ."

She let the tears come then. They coursed down
through her make-up—down, soaking into the white
dress.

The little man stood in front of her. Now he was
worried. For her. For himself. She was not usually
temperamental. He put one hand on her shoulder.
" You must go to bed, Elizabeth. You need to sleep.
You'll feel better in the morning. I will see you in the
morning. You had better take something to make
you sleep."

He put his hand to his waistcoat pocket. " Have
you anything? "

Elizabeth was drying her eyes. " Yes, I have something," she said tonelessly. " Sorry, Alex! "

He patted her shoulder. " It is nothing," he said.
" It is you I am worried about." He walked away and
collected his coat and hat from a chair. " I will come
to see you in the morning. Promise me you will go
to bed."

" I shall go to bed," she promised, like a child.

" Good-night," he said softly, and went out.

Elizabeth stood up. She walked across the room
and went to the bathroom. She took something from
the cabinet and took it into the sitting-room with a
glass of water. It was a small bottle. She opened it
and shook some tablets into her palm. She considered
them for a moment, then her eyes widened and quickly,
feverishly, she poured them all out until her hand was
full.

She stared at them as if she was in a trance. " No! "
I wanted to call out to her. " No, Elizabeth! Not
that! "

Then her whole body seemed to relax and slowly she poured them back again, all except two. I heaved a great sigh of relief. The picture faded.

4

It was ironic, really, that I eventually made planes after all. The war saw to that. All our factories and undertakings were geared to the war effort. It was impossible not to be even more prosperous than ever before.

But Fenton had to leave to go into the Army. I could, I think, have managed to keep him with me ; after all, he was on important work. But he wouldn't hear of it. He was rareing to go.

With him away as well as Elizabeth, the house seemed unnaturally quiet. And Walter was at college most of the time—though even when he was home we saw little of him.

Fenton's letters told us scarcely anything. Until he met Annette Marlow !

Annette, it seemed, was an assistant in a shop near where he was stationed. He didn't say how they had met, but it wasn't hard to visualise. Probably they had just got talking—a uniform seems to excuse many things that could not normally be done.

Fenton usually spoke so little about his affairs that it was obvious now that this girl had begun to mean something to him. Naturally the girl was interested ! Fenton was quite a passable fellow and once she knew who he was . . . well, there was plenty of incentive. And with a name like that—Annette ! It gave her away, almost.

I only hoped he would soon be moved to another camp. I had nothing against shop-girls. I was sure they were very nice people. But I didn't want Fenton to get mixed up with one.

And then he wrote again. He was due for leave. Could he bring Annette with him? He would like us to meet her.

Really, I thought, one can go too far! I replied and said that we saw so little of him, couldn't we have him to ourselves just over the leave? We were sure that Annette was a charming girl and all that he had said about her but we were certain she'd understand . . .

I didn't want to hurt the boy's feelings by saying any more.

I had barely posted my letter when a telegram came:

Terribly sorry, all leave cancelled. Moving on. Annette and I married yesterday. Very happy. Send your blessings. Love, Fenton.

Well, there it was! It was a great shock. But it was done and there was no way in which it could be undone. That was always the best and worst of a *fait accompli*.

" Well, fancy!" Janet said. " My boy married! I wonder what she's like."

" We won't even discuss it," I said, " because I don't want to lose my temper. One would think he might have done better than a shop-girl. But what worries me is this sudden move. It sounds as if he may be going overseas."

However, it was not to be yet. He wrote to say that Annette had given up her job and followed after him. He'd managed to get living quarters and they were both wonderfully happy.

My attention was diverted not long afterwards by the

news that Walter had been expelled from college in his first year.

He was quite unrepentant. He came in as though nothing untoward had happened, and I could feel my irritation increasing at that casual air of his. Why, I wondered, did I have to have a son like this? From the moment of his birth, when he had so nearly killed his mother, he had brought me nothing but trouble.

" Well? " I said.

He grinned. " Well what, Dad? " he drawled in that lazy way he had.

" Don't you think I'm entitled to an explanation? " I snapped. " Or are you proud of what you've done?"

He shrugged his shoulders and took out his cigarette-case. " What's the use? " he said and lit his cigarette. " It's over now. My saying I'm sorry isn't going to help any."

" I'd still like to know what happened."

" Oh, heck, it was nothing much. We just had a few drinks too many, I guess, and there were some girls around . . . They didn't have a lot of clothes on : seems we'd been playing strip poker . . ."

" I see. Drunk, rowdy, indecent and immoral— The College seems to have been well justified."

" Oh, for God's sake ! You make it sound like Sodom and Gomorrah. Like an old-time Evangelist."

I restrained myself patiently. " Look, Walter," I said. " You can't go on like this. Surely you realise that. I'm fairly wealthy and I suppose you think that I'll stand for everything you do. But I won't. I want all my children to start life with every possible advantage but I won't just stand by and see you waste your inheritance. And that's all you'll be fit for if you don't steady up now. And there's your mother. Don't you think this kind of thing hurts her? "

He had the grace to look a little shamefaced then. " Does she have to know? " he muttered.

" If you'll give me your word to settle down, well, perhaps she needn't know the details. What about it? "

" What do you want me to do? " he asked, his voice resigned.

" Well, I take it you don't want to go to another college? "

" No, I guess not."

" All right, then, how about a job? "

" A job? " he repeated as though the word was foreign to him. " You mean in an office? "

" Why not? People do work, you know."

" Oh, sure ! But— Who'd give me one, anyway? "

" I thought you might come into my business. It'll be yours, one day. You may as well learn how to run it. You and Fenton will have to do that after I've gone. You'll have to start at the bottom, of course. Like Fenton did."

He seemed bewildered. " I never thought I'd get myself into this. It's all right for Fenton—"

" Just what did you think you'd do after you left college? " I asked.

" I—well, I don't know. Just knock around for a while, I guess. After all we have got money, haven't we? What's the use of earning more? I thought maybe Fenton did it because he liked it. But me !—"

" Listen," I said. " I've built up the factory and the organisation. When someone does that he has a responsibility. And when he dies his family take over his responsibility. You'll be going into the Army soon enough. Meanwhile, why not get an idea of how things work, of planning and control? It'll be a start, anyway."

" But I know nothing about it. Nothing at all."

" You'll learn," I said grimly. " I'll see to that."

For a while I really thought Walter was going to settle down and make something of himself. Perhaps, I thought indulgently, I had been imagining him to be much worse than he was. Perhaps he had only been sowing wild oats—a little wilder to be sure than the usual variety—and was now about to turn into a respectable, hard-working citizen, a son of whom I could be proud.

He was conscientious over his work, I was informed, and his fellow-workers liked him ; he did not try to be heavy-handed with them as the boss's son : they would not have stood for that, and it was one mistake I had been afraid he would make. At home he stayed in quite a few nights and when he went out he came back again at a reasonable hour ; after all, I hardly wanted him to turn into an angel overnight : that would have been so unlikely that I would have had qualms about it.

" I think we may make something of your son yet," I said to Janet.

" Darling Walter ! " she said softly, smiling to herself. She never attempted to disguise from me her favouritism for him. " He's so good to me, and it's lovely to have him here. I don't know what I should do without him now."

The reversion was gradual. I suppose he simply could not keep it up ; his nature was against it.

Or was it simply that by then he had met Lois Manston?

It started with just a reversal of the previous process :
later nights, more nights spent out, later and later at
work in the mornings, some days away altogether . . .

The men under whom he worked were reluctant to
let me know how things were but they were not good
dissemblers and I soon screwed the truth out of them.

Thinking the matter over, I decided not to say
anything to him.   I would give him his head for a
while.   He might come back to heel if no one nagged
at him.   I wanted him to have every chance before
I had to pitch in to him.   Nor did I talk to Janet about
it.   But I could tell that she had an inkling of what
was going on.   Often I saw the worried look in her
eyes at Walter's absence night after night or his equally
ostentatious absence at breakfast, recovering, no doubt,
from a particularly long or hectic night out.   She did
not speak about it either and I knew why : she was
afraid to precipitate something from me.

There was no letting-up, though, and the time was
coming nearer when I should have to do something
about it.

The need for it never came ; something else came
instead.

Walter was arrested and held on a charge of attempted murder.

Frank Dawson came to tell me about it.   I knew
him quite well already.   He was a detective.

I had no inkling of his mission when he came to the
office that morning.   I did not connect his presence
with Walter's absence at all.   It was the first time
Walter had stayed out all night, and I had decided
then that things could not be left to drift on any longer.
But that was all.

" Well, hullo ! " I said.   " Haven't seen you for a long time. How's crime? Sit down and tell me all about it."

He sat down, refusing the cigar I offered him with a shake of his head. " Crime's not so good, I'm afraid."

" Oh, what's wrong with it? Too much or too little?"

He ignored my question and said casually : " How's that son of yours doing. The young one? "

" Walter? All right," I said.   The police wouldn't be interested in our domestic problems.

" Getting on well at the factory? "

" Oh, not too badly."

" Out at nights much, is he? "

" Quite a bit," I admitted unthinkingly. Then I frowned. " Look here, what's all this about? Walter's not in trouble, is he? "

He pushed out his lips.   " He spent last night in the caboose."

" Gaol? " I wasn't alarmed, only annoyed at what appeared to be another instance of Walter's trouble making.   " What was it, a raid on a night-club or something? One day he'll get in a mess that he can't get out of."

" This is that mess," Dawson said.   " Your son is charged with attempted murder."

My brain refused to accept it for a moment. Then the whole of my inside went cold. Instinctively I had been dreading something just like this for weeks though I had refused to believe it might really happen.

" Who was it? " I said.   " Why wasn't I told last night? I'm entitled to have a lawyer there before you cross-examine him . . ."

" Steady, Mr. Price ! It happened very late last

night and I thought maybe it would upset your wife if we roared in then with the news. You couldn't have done anything, anyway, and a night out in the cooler won't do your son any harm, if you don't mind my saying so. And we haven't grilled him. He made a voluntary statement."

My sense of importance collapsed. " Sorry," I said humbly. " It was thoughtful of you—about Mrs. Price. She would have been half out of her wits. What about the statement? Has he confessed? "

Thoughtfully, he said : " Not exactly. He admits shooting this bird—his name's Jenson McGrath—but he says it was self-defence. According to him there was a girl there, a night-club singer, name of Lois Manston. She's missing, and we'll have to find her. Meanwhile, we're holding him."

There was a chance then. A chance to get Walter out of this mess. But after that . . .

" There's nothing in the morning papers," I said.

" No, the story was too late for them. It'll make the mid-day papers, though. You couldn't stop it now, if that's what you're thinking."

A nice gory splash they'd make of it, I reflected bitterly. My fine son, Walter ! . . . I had been flirting with the idea of entering the political arena. My chance of that would be killed prematurely.

" I thought maybe you'd like to come along with me, Mr. Price. You could see your son."

" Thank you. I would, indeed."

From the story I got from Walter it was quite easy for me to picture the events as they must actually have happened.

Walter one day met up with a friend of his whom he

hadn't seen for some time. They decided to go to a night-club called " The Blue Lagoon " and have a drink to celebrate.

It was the usual kind of place. I suppose night-clubs anywhere differ but little. At least, they have much in common and " The Blue Lagoon " was of a one with a thousand others. It was clean and bright and blue was the predominating colour.

Walter and his friend Mark went up to the bar and drank and chatted for a while.

And then Lois Manston came out to sing.

Well, Lois Manston has been typed for us often enough by the cinema. Naturally she was pretty ; we can accept that without question. She was blonde and her figure was full and curving. But Walter said the hardness which is so often there was missing. Perhaps it was only hidden. He said there was something rather fresh and appealing about her. Perhaps, again, he was reading between the lines.

" She looks good enough to eat," he said admiringly to his friend.

Mark glanced at the girl. " You mean Lois? Oh, she's all right. Not my type."

Walter said eagerly : " Do you know her? "

" Yes, we've met a few times. Want to meet her? "

" Sure. But—"

" All right," he said casually. " I'll fetch her over after she's finished." He scribbled a note and gave it to a waiter for Lois with a tip for himself.

She came over. " Hullo, Mark," she said smiling. " Nice to see you again."

" How are you, Lois? I'd like you to meet a friend of mine—Mr. Walter Price."

" Hullo," she said, looking at him in that intimate

7

way that some women have.   Her voice had the warm, husky quality that singers often seem to have or affect. Her eyes were the lightest of blues—matching the general colour scheme.   Her tight evening gown, too, was powder-blue.

She had a couple of drinks with them and then she said she had to go.

" Oh, don't go yet," Walter protested.

He seemed particularly sincere about it and she looked at him with sudden interest.

" I'm due to sing another number.   I'll come back again if you like."

" That'll be fine."

Halfway through her number, Mark said he ought to be going.   Walter, not very politely perhaps, said : " Okay, Mark.   I'll just hang on a while, I think. Be seeing you."

Mark grinned at him.   " Be good," he said as he went off.

The girl came back and Walter bought some more drinks.   They began talking.

After a while Walter, gesturing round the room with his hand, asked : " Do you like this, singing here, and so on? "

The girl gave a little shrug.   " Could be worse, I guess.   What do you do, Wally? "

He grinned, slightly shamefaced.   " I just work. At my father's factory.   Just learning, I guess he'd call it.   And not very quickly, either."

" What does your father do? "

" Oh, the Pridex works and all that."

" You mean your father is Dexter Price? "   Couldn't he see her eyes light up with interest?

" Yes, that's right.   You've heard of him.   Everyone has, I suppose. That's what success does for you. A great thing success, Lois. You ought to hear my father talking about it: it's an experience."

" It must be," she said softly.

She spent the rest of her time between songs with him and then he asked if he could take her home.

She glanced at him as if the notion was new to her. " Yes," she said in her warm way, " that'll be lovely."

As she stood up she looked meaningly at someone across the floor, flashing a message from those pale blue eyes. Walter saw nothing.

" I'll get my wrap," she said. She did, but there was also a little conversation with a large, snaky-looking man out of sight of where Walter was waiting.

She came back with her wrap and he drove her to her apartment.

" Would you like to come in for a moment and have a drink? "

The husky voice was sure of the answer even as it made the invitation.

They had the drink. Her fingers, her knee, her foot—all managed accidentally to touch Walter's. She was certainly an attractive girl—and very close. Walter suddenly kissed her. She struggled—but not enough to break his hold. Then she acquiesced. Finally, quite a time later, she struggled again and broke away.

" No," she said. " No, it's not fair, Wally."

" What's not fair? " Why did women always want to have a discussion at the wrong times?

" There's something I haven't told you. I'm married."

" Married? " He stood up and lit a cigarette.

" Yes, Manston's my own name. I'm really Mrs.

Jenson McGrath. Jenson and I—we don't hit it off
very well. He doesn't live here. Not really. Just
comes back when he feels like it. I hate him. But
what can I do? I'm—I'm frightened of him."

Walter frowned. " You don't have to stay here.
He can't force you to."

She shivered realistically. " I tell you, I'm frightened of him, Wally. He doesn't want me, really.
Just likes to feel he owns me. I don't know why he
married me. I was pretty raw ; he took me around,
gave me a good time . . ."

She smiled. " I am sorry, Wally. I thought you
ought to know."

" You poor kid ! " he said, forgetting that she was
undoubtedly older than he was.

" He's threatened me once or twice when I've told
him I want a divorce. He's a tough sort of fellow—a
professional gambler. He said if I divorced him he'd
get me, that I was his property, and he never let go
of what was his."

Mr. McGrath sounds a nice sort of person," Walter
said. " I'd like to meet him."

" No, no, please ! " She stood up and put her hand
earnestly on his arm. " I'd be afraid something might
happen."

Walter put his arms round her. " Listen, honey,"
he said. " You need looking after. We'll have to
think about your Jenson seriously."

" Oh," she said, looking tenderly up at him. " I
am glad I met you, Wally."

Somewhat naturally he kissed her.

She pushed him away after a while. " Go now,
Wally," she begged. " Please."

" You're not scared of me ? " he said.

" No, I'm scared of myself. So—you'd better go
now. But come again soon. If you want to."

" Will to-morrow do? " Walter asked, sure of himself now.

" All right, to-morrow then. At the club."

That was the first of many visits, both to the night-
club and to her apartment. She continued to accept
his sympathy in its most practical manifestation, but
always restraining him from too hectic love-making.
She held him off whilst yet managing to urge him ever
onwards with unspoken promises, binding him more
and more surely.

The small scheme might have been hurried with the
same result, but they preferred to take it slowly. They
wanted to make certain and also to choose the most
opportune time. Apart from which Lois was acquiring
some useful presents from the boy.

At last they decided to operate. Lois had made
certain that Walter would go to the club that night.
And when it was time to close he took her home as
he had often done before. Perversely he wanted to
leave her for once and go home. He was feeling
tired, he said. She coaxed him.

" You're always leaving me," she protested.

" You always make me," he retorted.

" Darling, how would you like not to have to go
away to-night? " Her eyes were inviting as she leaned
towards him.

" Lois, do you really mean that? "

" Come in and see," she said.

Immediately he was inside he became ardent. But
he was too previous. " Wait," she said, laughing. " I
must go and change." She vanished into the bedroom.

After a while he heard her calling him softly. She stood in the bedroom doorway in a negligee.

" How do I look ? " she said.

She looked soft and warm and desirable, but she didn't need to be told that. When he went over to her she retreated. He followed. He caught her, kissed her wildly and, picking her up, carried her to the bed.

A minute later the door opened with a jerk. They both looked up, startled, towards it and there was a flash. The smaller of two men, holding a camera and flash-bulb, detached himself quickly from the doorway and bolted. The other man, a large snaky fellow, came forward.

Lois' eyes widened with simulated alarm. " Jenson ! " she said, her voice small and frightened.

" Well," he said viciously, " so I've caught you at last ! And Mr. Walter dirty Price ! "

Walter, having recovered himself to some extent, said : " So this is your husband ! I've been wanting to meet you."

" This is your big chance," the man said. " Brother, you've got some quick explaining to do—or some cash to pay."

" Meaning what ? "

" Meaning that I want a nice big cheque or that photograph will be handed straight to Daddy Price. And that would make good entertainment for him, wouldn't it? And I'll have a story to go with it—a divorce. I could make it a good story ; I've been here before when you were here—and not alone."

" All right—let it go," Walter said. He turned to Lois. " My father won't be exactly crazy about it. But this is your chance to get that divorce of yours. Then we can get married."

"Oh no, Wally," said Lois quickly. "Not this way. Please. I couldn't take it. I'd never be able to get a job again. Please do what he asks. Money doesn't mean an awful lot to you . . ." She began to cry.

McGrath spoiled it then, just when Walter might have given in. "You noble little fellow!" he sneered.

Walter clenched his jaw. "Blast you!" he said, and went at him. He got one blow to McGrath's face and then the other managed to push him off.

McGrath's hand went into a pocket and came out with a gun. "Keep back!" he snarled. "I thought this might be handy."

Walter thoroughly infuriated by now, ignored the revolver and leapt forward. They both struggled madly for possession of the revolver. Walter was forcing McGrath's hand to bend. McGrath must have had his finger round the trigger. Suddenly the gun went off and McGrath collapsed, groaning to the floor. After a moment he lost consciousness.

Walter stood stupefied, but it was Lois who startled him most. She gave a scream and then rushed across to McGrath. "Jen!" she cried. "Jen! Are you all right. For Christ's sake, darling!" She held up his head and looked viciously at Walter. "You little toad!" she said. "You've killed him, my husband. By God—do you think I'd leave a man like him for a little rat like you? You fool, fool . . ."

Dazed by the sequence of events and yet seeing only one fact emerge clearly—that Lois had been in on the blackmailing affair with McGrath—Walter walked slowly out of the apartment. He left his hat behind, but the police would have got him anyway. Lois' voice, screaming remarks after him, followed him out.

Then, thinking McGrath was dead, and terrified of being found alone with him, she herself ran out.

When the police came—the shot had been reported —they found McGrath groaning again and the gun beside him. He thought he was dying, but he hated the idea of going without implicating Walter.

"He's been after my wife for some time," he said weakly. "He wanted me out of the way, pulled a gun on me . . ."

After I'd finished talking to Walter I saw Inspector Dawson again. "What about this photographer?" I asked. "He might be able to tell us something."

"Yes, I've seen him. He corroborates Walter's story as far as he can. But he left pretty early. He says he was almost certain that McGrath had a gun in his pocket."

"You must find the girl," I said.

They did find her, two days later. She was too frightened to do anything but tell the truth. It was self-defence all right and they let Walter go. They telephoned me and I asked them to hold him until I got there.

I took a case with some of his clothing in and I asked if I could see him alone.

"Well, you're out of it," I said. "By the skin of your teeth. We've had enough publicity and scandal over this to last us the rest of our lives. You're a disgrace to the family and you've been heading this way all your life."

It was the first time I had seen Walter look shaken over something I'd said to him. "But, Dad—how did I know I was being made a fool of? I thought the girl was terrified—"

" I don't want to discuss it," I said coldly. " It's all over now. I don't care what happened : the very fact that anything happened is enough. Your poor mother—well, never mind now ! The point is this. As long as you stay round here you're going to bring nothing but trouble. I've brought you some clothes and here's a good-sized cheque."

He stood staring at me.

" What I'm trying to say is that I don't want to spend the rest of my life wondering what I shall read next about you in the paper when I pick it up. What I want you to do is to go away. As far away as you can. Perhaps you'll make good on your own. I don't know. You never will here. And I can't accept any more responsibility for you. I think it will be best if we don't hear from you. Letters will only upset your mother. That's all I have to say—except good-bye."

I thought he was going to speak. Then he thrust the cheque in his pocket, picked up the bag and hurried from the room without a word or another look.

I told Janet that Walter had just left of his own accord. But she was suspicious : she wouldn't believe that he could just go away without first seeing her. She kept on at me until, in a fit of temper, I admitted that I'd sent him packing.

" Dexter, I'll never forgive you. That poor boy ! Your own son ! How could you do it ? "

" He was bad all through," I said.

" He was not. He only wanted understanding and patience. But you never offered him either, only your irritability and anger—always throwing your ' success ' in his face. I could have helped him as no one else

can. And we don't even know where he is ! Oh,
Walter, what have we done? "

She went upstairs, weeping. She cried for days,
starting again without any warning. I was really
alarmed ; I had never seen her like that before.

" Don't worry about him so," I said. " He'll
probably be quite all right. He may do very well
now he's got to stand on his own two feet."

She refused even to discuss him with me any more.

It was soon after that she had her first bad illness.

Now I had an unexpected glimpse of Walter. He
was in a bar, a very dirty bar, it seemed. The only
furniture consisted of a few rough tables and chairs.
The walls were a dull brown but stained and
filthy. From the people there it appeared to be in a
Latin-American country. Walter was drinking at the
bar. Whatever it was he was drinking he slopped out
of his glass whenever he drank ; his hand was shaking
badly. He, too, was dirty. His face was unshaven
and he seemed to have aged about twenty years.
There were lines and pouches, slack flesh and a mean,
vicious expression. His clothes were shabby and
neglected.

There was a card game in progress across the room
and, noticing it, Walter staggered over to it. He pulled
up a chair with his foot—almost overbalancing in the
attempt—and pushed his way into the game. The
other players looked at each other and shrugged their
shoulders. They didn't mind ; he could obviously do
nothing but lose money in the state he was in. And
so it was, Walter becoming more and more drunken, a
slatternly girl bringing fresh drinks to him periodically.

Suddenly he stretched out his hand to play and fell

flat on his face, dead drunk. The others laughed. Calmly they rifled his pockets, then they carried him haphazardly outside, dumping him ungently on the ground.

The slatternly girl, laughing, brought his hat to the door and threw it out after him. They all went back, still laughing.

The picture was, to me, almost unbearable, but just then it faded.

5

Janet had her second bad illness just after we had the telegram giving news of Fenton's death in action. From then on she had periodic spells in bed.

His death was a terrible blow to me, too—one of the greatest I had ever had to bear.

Janet had been corresponding with his wife, Annette, sporadically and soon afterwards she told us she was expecting a child. We were both excited at once at the prospect of a grandchild.

"Annette must come and stay here," Janet said. " She can have the baby here and have the best attention—and they can both live here. It will be like Fenton growing up again." I hadn't seen her so excited for months.

" It may be a girl," I said.

" Whatever it is, there will be something of Fenton in it."

I agreed with her suggestion. I was not anxious to have the girl herself, but I supposed I should have to put up with the one to get the other. With Fenton gone and Walter out of the running there was no one to put into the business to keep on my name. Perhaps this would be the answer. I, too was quite excited.

I let Janet arrange it all. I didn't want to have more to do with it than I could help.

When Annette arrived I had to admit she was quite different to my conception of her. On the whole she seemed a sensible girl, neither flashy as I had feared, nor grasping, as I had expected. I asked her where she had got her name from and she said her mother had been French. But she had been brought up over here and there was nothing French about her now except a certain chicness. She was a nice-looking girl and she had a cool independence about her that was rather attractive—at first ; later it became irritating and proved itself to be merely stubbornness.

Perhaps I had been wrong about it being Fenton's money that had attracted her. I could see why Fenton had fallen for her and perhaps after all they had been genuinely in love.

She settled down in the household calmly and with self-possession. Her only complaint was that everything was done for her and that she had too little to do herself ; she was not used to that.

" Don't you bother yourself about that, dear," Janet told her. " Your job is to have your baby. That's something we can't do for you, anyway."

Annette smiled. " I'm glad I'm having the baby. It's not quite so bad as if he'd left me with—nothing, nothing but a few lovely months."

Janet smiled back. " We're all glad and glad to have you here too so that we can all share a little in the baby."

" We musn't turn his head," Annette said, " with too much attention."

I hoped, indeed, that it would be a ' he '.

And so it was. James Fenton Price he was named, but we all called him Fenton ; one was glad to be using the name again.

He was a fine lad and we showered him with toys and attention. I suppose he did get a little spoilt. I began to be afraid of the probability and reaction swung me the other way. I was scared that too much indulgence might turn him into a second Walter. Though I loved him dearly I treated him quite sternly almost from the time he began to talk. I don't mean with real unyielding sternness, and perhaps " firmness " would be the better word.

We had a nurse for him, an excellent woman with all sorts of diplomas and recommendations. Annette said she didn't care for her much but I told her that was nonsense ; I had personally selected her from dozens of applicants. Janet was not too well just then, and in any case I wanted to be sure that we employed the best obtainable. Annette said she didn't want a nurse at all for young Fenton and that, I said, really was nonsense. Just being a mother doesn't necessarily qualify one for bringing up a child the best way and this woman was an expert.

" He's my child," Annette said.

" He's my grandson," I returned. " And I want him to have the best of everything all his life. He's going to have a lot of responsibility one day and training starts now ; there's no age too young for that."

" Training for what ? " she asked sarcastically. " A successful business man ? I don't want a business man in the making for a son. I just want a normal boy, someone to love and look after."

" That's a very selfish point of view."

" Is it?   I don't think so."

" Who are you thinking of? The boy or yourself? "

" Who are *you* thinking of? " she flung back at me.

I stared silently at her.   How could she doubt that I had the boy's interests at heart?

" Oh, listen," she said.   " I don't want to quarrel with you.   I dare say really you do mean well for Fenton.   I just think differently about him and how he should be brought up.   That's all there is to it. But we'll give your way a trial if you like.   That's the fairest thing."

But minor points of disagreement were always cropping up.   The nurse knew that Annette did not like her and Annette was always interfering with her methods and routine.   Which I considered wrong, since I knew that if one wanted an expert's advice one did not go against that advice on every possible occasion.   Since I had employed the nurse she naturally came to me with her complaints and, naturally, I backed her up.

One evening she came to see me in tears.   I was in my study.

" Well, Nurse," I said, surprised.   " What's all this about? "

" I'm leaving, Mr. Price.   I'm leaving this very instant.   I'll not stay in this house a minute longer."

" Come now," I said, " don't be impulsive.   What's happened? "

" Well, it's Mrs. Annette again.   It started about Fenton's bath.   I was about to give him one as usual when along she comes.   ' No bath,' she says, ' not with Fenton having a cold '."   I told her it wasn't much of a cold at all and a bath wouldn't hurt him in the slightest.   She said she wasn't going to risk it anyway, and I told her that I was a qualified nurse and I wouldn't give him a bath if I thought there was any risk. So then she started, saying she'd had enough of it and wasn't going to stand any more; she was the boy's mother and if she couldn't look after her own child it was about time she changed the methods in this house. She—she called me a lot of names and said that I was probably very competent but she didn't want me, competent or not. If I didn't leave she would, and the quicker I went the better she'd be pleased. Well, Mr. Price, I'm not standing that sort of treatment from anyone."

"Now calm down," I said. "We'll straighten this out all right."

"No, I'm sorry but I'm not changing my mind. Not this time. I'm going where my services will be appreciated. It's not your fault, I know, Mr. Price. You've done all you could to help. But I wouldn't stay now if Mrs. Annette begged me." She began to sniff again, and went out.

I rang for Johnson, the butler, and asked him to find Mrs. Annette for me—we called her that to differentiate between her and Janet.

He returned a few minutes later with the surprising message that: "Mrs. Annette regrets she is unable to come to your study, sir. She says that she will be glad to see you in her room if you care to go."

I controlled my temper. "I see. Very well, Johnson, thank you."

"Yes, sir."

I went to Annette's room. Insufferable girl, making me look ridiculous before the servants! I knocked and went in.

" Sorry if it was asking you too much to come to see me," I said.

" I won't be sent for like a schoolgirl to be given a row about that damned nurse."

" She says she's leaving. I can't make her change her mind. I think you ought to apologise to her."

She strode towards me and stood with her hands on her rather shapely hips. " You do, do you? Well, let me tell you something. I meant every word I said to her. And if she doesn't leave, I will."

" You're being unreasonable, Annette. She's an excellent nurse. It'll be hard to find another as good."

" Which brings me to something else," she said determinedly. " There won't be another nurse."

" Now, don't be foolish. Of course we must have a nurse."

" Listen," she said, " and please think carefully. I say I will not have another nurse. Are you going to fight me over it? "

I gestured with my hand and gave a short laugh. " If you make me fight you I shall have to, I suppose. But yes, I'm serious about it if that's what you mean."

" Right ! " she exclaimed. " That settles it. I know now that it won't only be the nurse ; later it'll be schools, doctors, illnesses, holidays—everything. You'll always want your own way and I shall always want mine. Only he's my son and I shall have my way."

" What on earth are you talking about, Annette? We wouldn't have to disagree if only you were reasonable—"

" Meaning if I agreed with you? Well, I'm not staying to find out, Mr. Dexter Price. I'm leaving. With Fenton."

She pulled out a suitcase from a cupboard. " We'll leave first thing in the morning."

I looked aghast at her ; she was obviously serious.

" Now you are being selfish," I told her angrily. " Think of all the advantages I can give him. You haven't any money ; I know Fenton hadn't much of his own to leave you. What will you live on? "

" We'll manage," she said in that independent way of hers, beginning to pack, " even if I have to go out to work."

" In a shop again," I sneered. " A fine job for Fenton's mother ! "

She turned round. Her voice sounded as if it had been compressed. " I think you've said quite enough. Would you please get out of my room? "

I could not believe that she would really go. Before I went to sleep that night I decided to reason with her again in the morning.

But when I got up she and Fenton had already left.

I was furious. I hadn't even any address for her. I put some private detectives on her track and they found her for me. She and Fenton were living in a small apartment.

I went to see her.

" Well," she said coolly. " So you've found me. Have you been playing sleuths or did you have a real detective? "

" There's no need to be rude, surely. You gave us no address, so I had to trace you. How is the boy? "

" Very well. Much better off than he ever was under your nurse."

" May I see him? "

She considered, and then brought him in.

He was shy because he had not seen me for a while.

" Hullo, Fenton. Are you having fun? Does your mummy take you to the park? Wouldn't you like to come back and live with Granny and Grandad again? In the big house like you used to? "

" That's not fair," she flashed.

" Want to stay with Mummy," the child said.

" Listen, son. Don't you remember all those big toys of yours—the bear and the horse and the bird that sings? Wouldn't you like to have them again? "

He stared mutely at me.

" That's all," Annette broke in. " Run along, darling. I'll come to see you in a little while. And now," she said when he had gone, " you can deal with someone your own size, who won't be taken in by your blandishments."

" You're angry, aren't you? "

" Of course I am. I don't like the way you set about things. You think everyone and everything is to be bought."

" Mostly they are."

" Well, I'm not. And my son's not. I know you're his grandfather but that doesn't give you the right to order his life."

" You're not making it easy for me. I'd like you to come back, Annette."

" And start all over again? No, I've made up my mind now that this is the best way. I'll bring him to see you now and then, of course. Unless I decide to move."

" You mean you might go away? "

" Yes, some time. Why not? "

" But you can't do that. We'd never see him. I won't let you."

Her eyes widened. " I can do whatever I like. That's just what I'm trying to get you to understand. And if you think I'm going to mortgage his whole life for a grub-stake in your miserable factory, you're wrong."

I curbed myself. " All right," I said. " We shall see."

To the detectives I said : " I want my grandson back. He'll be my heir if I have the custody of him, and obviously it will be to his advantage in every way. I can give him everything ; his mother, nothing. But that won't be enough for a Court. They like some- thing better than that, some evidence that she wouldn't make a good mother. You know what I mean—there must be something in the girl's life. If there isn't yet, there will be some time ; a girl like that won't want to live alone for ever. Even if she wanted to she wouldn't get the chance : she's too good looking. Maybe there's something in her past, too. If there is, dig it up. I'll leave it to you."

" If there isn't anything do you want evidence planted? "

There seemed to be few scruples amongst some of the members of this trade.

" I don't like the question," I said. " I've told you what I require if you can get it. The rest's up to you."

There wasn't much about her past that was any good to me. A few flirtations, romances—but nothing serious before Fenton.

I began to despair of success, too, in the present. But the opportunity came at last, falling unexpectedly right into our laps.

A young man had visited Annette one evening. He

had stayed, according to the watching detective, until the following morning. He was dressed in Army uniform.

It was enough. Quickly I got in touch with my lawyer and we slapped in an application for custody of the child.

The story Annette, apparently bewildered by the turn of events, told in Court was that the young man, a friend of both hers and Fenton's and who had known them both when they had got married, had traced her through mutual friends and had gone to look her up. He had been rather a special friend of Fenton's. They talked about past times and then the young man disclosed that he had nowhere to stay. He had already tramped the streets looking for a hotel for the night without success. He was moving on the next day, and Annette, sorry for him, offered him a shakedown for the night in her apartment. She hadn't thought anything of it at the time.

Though I personally believed her story, my lawyer in Court poured scorn on it. Was it likely, he asked, that an attractive young girl, awakened by marriage and then so tragically widowed, was it likely that she and this young man would spend the night together and nothing happen? And he had come along especially to see her. Just for friendship's sake? Well, really, one could only swallow so much! And if with this young man, who knew with what others as well?

I felt quite sorry for the girl. She was crying. For her wickedness, perhaps, the Court might think!

The Court wisely refrained from passing any specific judgment on her morals. It considered that in the circumstances the advantages I could offer the child weighed in my favour. And if she had to go out to work it would only handicap her considerably in her efforts to look after the child properly.   No doubt she wanted what was best for the child?   The question came gently.

"Of course, but—" she bit her lip.

The custody of the child was awarded to me.

A great agonised cry hurled itself across the Court. "No! No!"

Someone beside her touched her, restraining her. She went out weeping, her head shaking, telling herself that it wasn't true.

Fenton, back with us, cried a great deal at first and called incessantly for his mother.   It was only to be expected.   But when he got over that he seemed to have lost the bright eagerness he had always had before, the air that life was a great and wonderful adventure.   He was completely apathetic.   Yet never would I admit to myself that there was any connection between this attitude and his mother's continued absence.   Annette had never been to see him since the day of the Court order.   She wrote to me one letter only, in bitter vein, renouncing him, so she said, to the Government and to God-at-any-Price . . .

6

The small screen in my mind went blank and then dark.   The horribly unyielding review of some of the highlights in my life seemed to be over.   I sat stunned and still.

I felt quite sick and my head was throbbing.   I kept my eyes closed.   How long had the experience taken? A couple of hours? A few minutes? I could not tell.

I didn't even care ; I was long past caring about time. I felt as if I had been stripped naked and paraded before a group of people. But it had been immeasurably worse : I had been shown to myself ; and the nakedness had been inside. There, I was raw and quivering ; I had glimpsed a soul, my own. I had seen myself as others had seen me—which is much the same thing, for we may often see a man's soul peeping out of himself, never our own. Sometimes it is raw and ugly, sometimes bright and shining ; more often a mixture of both. Mine was raw and ugly.

What was it Death had called me? Selfish, greedy, mean, possessive, conceited, cruel and lustful. . . . How true it was I had just seen for myself. True every one of those adjectives and every one I would have denied only a short time before—had, in fact, done so. If only I had been able to see myself before ! I had deluded myself that all I did was for others, yet I knew now that it had all been for myself, to satisfy the hunger of my own ego in the name of others. I had called my thoughtlessness, my self-seeking, by high-sounding names : a desire to help, doing what I believed to be best . . . Best for whom, I wondered now?

That fellow I had seen playing the scenes in my mind's eye—I knew him to be myself and yet he seemed strangely unlike my own conception of myself, the one I had lived with for so long, believing him to be a fine, honest, upstanding person, one—had I not said it myself ?—who had never done anything to be ashamed of.

My importance had burst like a cracked tomato ; no longer did I want to plead for more time . . .

" You're right," I said aloud. " The world will

lose nothing by my going : it can only gain.   I'm quite
ready now.   I apologise for keeping you waiting."

I opened my eyes.   I wished it wasn't quite so dark,
so that I could see where I was going.   It was more like
a fog than simply darkness.   But there, it was beginning
to clear.   I started to struggle up.

"Dex, what is it?" I heard Janet's voice calling,
alarmed.

The fog cleared completely and I looked up to find
Janet hovering over me, her quilted dressing-gown
tightly round her, her eyes gazing at me with concern.

I looked quickly past her, towards the carved chair
at my desk.   It was empty.   My eyes ran round the
room ; there was no one else there.   But—

And then I understood.   Without wanting time, I
had been granted it.   But it would not be for the purpose I had originally sought it, to aggrandise myself
still more, to bolster my importance into a suitable
memorial before I departed, to parcel out my little
empire so that it would not fall to pieces when I
died. . . .   My very realisation of my uselessness had
transformed it.

"Dex—you're ill."

"Ill?" I said.   I stood up.   "Ill?" I laughed.
"No, I'm not ill.   I'm gloriously well."

"I was worried," she said.   "It was so late.   I.
thought I heard you come in a long time ago.   But
you didn't come up.   I wondered if anything had
happened.   Was the dinner a successs?"

"The dinner?" How far away that seemed.   "Oh,
yes, the dinner.   Yes, it was all right." How unim-
portant the plaudits sounded now.   "Janet, am I
very old?"

"No, dear, you're fifty—"

" I don't mean the age.   I mean, there's still a lot I can do, isn't there? "

" Oh, yes, I suppose so."   A quirk touched her lips. " Still striving for the moon? Yes, I daresay you can find new worlds to conquer. Is that what you've been planning? "

" No," I said.   " I was thinking about other things, important things."

Oh, the pity of it, that it took me all these years to find out what things were important, to be able to put things in their proper perspective ! Yet some people never did reach that stage . . .   There was, after all, still much good I could do.   I had boasted that money could do most things ; now it could be put to the test. And I had, besides, to help me, power and position— and time, all the rest of my earthly time.   Things done could not be all undone—that is the tragedy of late knowledge—but Elizabeth—Walter—Annette—surely I could help those to some sort of happiness just as I had helped them to unhappiness.   I could never make up what was spent, but could I not bring them recompense of some kind? It might not be too late to bring them and others a measure of peace.   And for Janet, too, I could work to bring contentment, Janet who had stood by so loyally and for so long even though she had seen many things to distress her, even though I had all but broken her heart twice, and perhaps more. She deserved so much more than the Dexter Price I had met to-night, the one she had lived with all these years.   For others, also, strangers as yet, I had the means and the opportunity to do much . . .

I suddenly remembered that Janet was ill, ought not to be there.   " You shouldn't have come down," I said gently.

" I'm all right. I feel a little better for being up.
But you— There's something strange about you
to-night. What have you been doing down here?
Not worrying about anything? "

" No. I looked in a mirror and met a man—someone
you know. I thought he was an old friend of mine,
too, but he was a stranger. I went into the mirror
and he showed me his life."

" Dex, you're talking so strangely. It's so unlike
you. Who was this man? Did you have a dream? "

" A dream? Perhaps. A dream of a spirit, the
terrible self-seeking spirit eating out the heart of the
world. Janet, it's so easy to live with one's conscience
half-asleep—like a sentry staring always ahead and
being stabbed in the back. There are so many things
most of us do unthinkingly, selfishly. Yet the forgotten
moment never returns. If we saw it again we might
hate it, so we kill it and bury it quickly, trundling it
off to eternity in all its hideousness. The dark moment
must be hidden because otherwise it might sicken us.
We might see it as it really was, not as we made ourselves believe it was. But perhaps, the future . . .
one can always look to that. To forget ourselves and
our own desires! Is that possible, Janet? My God,
what a small ambition!—Yet we can't achieve it.
But one day that small ambition will girdle the earth—
perhaps fashion the world a soul! . . ."

Janet turned to me. A delighted smile lit up her
face. " Why, Dex, darling—and I thought I knew
you inside out after all this time! "

I put my arm round her shoulders. " Let's go to
bed," I said. " I seem to have had rather an exciting
evening."